Sunny Disposition:

An Anthology of Florida Authors

Edited by Michael Paul Anthony and Shane T. Spiker

First edition in November 2021.

Book Design by WND Press, LLC

Published by WND Press, LLC

ISBN: 978-1-7948-1850-1

Acknowledgements

We would like to take a second to thank all of the Florida authors that contributed to this work. This place is weird but beautiful, and it's not easy to capture in writing. Thank you for being vulnerable and representing our strange swamp.

Table of Contents

A Note from the Editors: Sunny Disposition.

Florida. What a strange place. When my compatriot and I decided to start WND Press, our most important value was to ensure that we took care of authors and creative folks working with us. This company has been a DIY project from the start, with the aim to find a place for those folks who wanted to create but didn't have the resources or access to large publishers. We know we aren't the first to do this, and there are probably some publishers out there who do it better. We can acknowledge our faults. But for all of our faults, we have a passion for continuing the creative pursuit, and encouraging others to do the same.

Both of us come from punk rock, where being creative, or at least DOING something creative, was as simple as picking up a guitar and strumming a few chords. It wasn't perfect. We weren't trained. And most of the time we just made noise. But there was beauty in the process. And while we might not have written the next *Rocket to Russia* or *Damaged*, we certainly tried to write what we loved.

Writing isn't much different, when you think about it. How many times have you sat down to write, only to kill your darlings? To ball up the paper and throw it in the trash, losing it to eternity? I've done it, and I know for a fact others involved in this project have done the same. But sometimes the pursuit is where we find the beauty.

The authors in this work are all from Florida. They hail from here, or spent enough time here to have some experience with the sweltering heat and uncompromising strangeness that defines the state. Here, we recognize Floridians are a different breed, for better or worse. We have our stuff, and we're home to the world's worst superhero, Florida Man. But for some of us, there is a deep, enduring love for this place. I can't speak for the other authors in this book, but personally, I wouldn't call anywhere else home.

We wanted to put together this book to highlight those creatives, who continued to persevere after throwing away their work. To highlight those who wanted to share their work, and were brave enough to allow the world to see it. In this collection, we share stories of fiction and non-fiction as well as some poems. Some are funny, and some are dark. The variety itself is indicative of the diversity in our state. So as you begin to move through this book, please know that there are multiple aims:

1. Collect works from people who dared to be creative.
2. Share some of the variety that exists in our beautiful state.
3. Provide an outlet for writers and creatives by lifting their voices.
4. Have fun

After all, creative pursuits are exactly that; fun. They are explorations of the depths of humanity that other practices cannot begin to touch.

Please enjoy this collection of works we lovingly titled Sunny Disposition. And if you are a writer, do not stop. Continue the work, because sometimes the magic is in the process, not the product.

Shane and Michael

Christian Bradt

Costa Rica 1

Let's be frank;
there are crabs hiding
behind the toilet
and I am drunk.
I have not even looked at
the night sky
until now.

Let's be honest;
I'm afraid to carry life
and that my sister cannot
and these things are parameters
for living with loss.
There is a millipede
in the shower
and I do not know the way
back to you.

Kumquats

The light spreads horizontal
and the day grows swollen.
I find feathers of an everyday bird
with no blood on them
while picking fruit from your tree.
All of a Sunday!
Water runs through my bony-linked fingers,
my thumbs rub the womb-round creations.
You and your rhythms from the other room,
Me and my wonder
and hands full of flesh,
usual idols
and sometimes gods.

Michelle's Lumpectomy

I am not so ready as a knife
to part our bodies.
A stone between us
would be crippling cold.
Our years of drowning
cannot finally overtake the heat of sand
seeping into our bones
during our hour holidays.
Why should the salt in your blood
not keep you floating still?
That dark seed cannot
cannot, cannot
cool you.
Those roots can't pull you back down
away from my tiny hands.

For Oscar on a Hard Morning

A morning slow lizard
on a primordial burst orange.
Your curled tongue
set for ruinous joy.
You will proclaim yourself wildly
to everything.
Me with my misanthropic
hangdog mien.
With an arm pulled taught
at an angle proscribed by
your relationship with every smell
in the world.
My arm an extension of you.
Me, no more than a tether.

I Shotgunned a Beer in the Parking Lot When I got the Call You Relapsed

The indignity of rotting
from the inside out...
the way of it should be a slow
tiring of life, mind first.
A wearing of the years.
Or quick
before the realization
that there will never be anything new,
not ever again.
But to *be* new,
to see around the corner
the new anything-at-all,
to go after it
trailing fingernails
bowels
hair...
this is not the way.
This is not the way life can know itself.
This is not the way I
can accept you dying,
in patches of skin,
in one more food you cannot
eat anymore;
in percentages
when you are a wholeness.
A whole life
happening and
ending.
All at once.

What I Left You For

"Todavía no?" you asked
about something other than
what we should have been talking about.?
Right then, we hollowed out the present
and filled a number of possible futures.
Right then,
in the middle of everything else,
-the potato salad, the beer, the breeze-
without changing the course
of even the conversation
those moments were suddenly revealed
and they were now.
"Not yet," I said.
But I could not unsee what was seen.
Other selves living other possible lives,
now, alongside us,
every decision made one way
also being made another.

A Family Affair

He saw the yellow towel, first. At least that's what he would tell people in the version that would become automatic, reflexive over time. That version of the story of a tragedy that has enough strange and disparaging detail to flatter the listener that the teller is baring themselves, and so must be the truest version. Yellow, in a shade of Easter pastel that only certain kinds of wives would pick and so reminded him irritatingly of his ex-wife, the reminder wedging her, intruding and asserting themselves into his thoughts, even now.

In the truest version that he was ashamed to admit to even himself, though, he took in the towel in the same near instantaneous sweep his brain took to survey the scene and assess the potential threats in a room. His face betraying no reaction. These are the skills he learned guarding prisoners for twenty years. He took it in and his actual first thought was: "of course. It was always going to be this way." Some part of him expected the worst, at every moment, in the most mundane and beautiful things. Even from his son. His beautiful, beautiful son.

So his reaction on opening the door was a tightening of the mouth, his already-thin lips disappearing in a straight, white, grim line, and a sharp rushing of air out of his nostrils as if he had been holding a breath. But the next instant he was sure he'd never breathe deeply again, and the grief and horror escaped in a guttural howl. Hands outstretched, he was frozen in place, totally unable to reach out and touch his son.

His son was beyond touch, beyond help. The yellow hand towel was draped over the top of the boy's head, a grotesque and thoughtful gesture meant to minimize the mess his father would have to clean up. There was strangely little blood on the parts of the towel the man could see, but the boy had not understood the mechanics of a self-inflicted gunshot wound to the roof of the mouth, and his effort to contain the spatter failed resulting in details his father would relive until he himself gave up living. The fragmentation of the bullet blended his brain and forced it out of the damaged ear canals and open mouth. It had clotted and dripped black onto the gold varsity letter on his jacket. It dripped from the well-organized shelving propping his slumped body, half sitting in a dark mimicry of his normal teenage slouch. As if he would suddenly lunge forward full of his barking laughter at the joke.

In the same sweep his father also saw the cell phone on the shelf, the book light, still on, illuminating the open notebook and pen set carefully on the floor at a distance meant to keep the paper clean, the note safety pinned to his boy's jacket that said "read first" and was somehow free of blood. He saw the gun. His gun. His home defense automatic pistol the boy showed so little interest in that he lazily left it out when he exchanged it for his state-issued sidearm on his way out the door for work every night. To save himself the hassle of the safe, when the boy had gotten old enough to trust. One casing, shining on the floor.

He mechanically retraced his steps along a path now full of ominous markers. The garage door, slightly open. The back door, unlocked. The cheerful bathroom nightlight the boy never used, on. The bedroom door, wide open with no boy in the bed and the strange gift bags on top of the blanket. The laptop on the nightstand, still open where it had been when he said goodnight to his son. He even shut the front door on his way out of the house and stood next to his truck, keys somehow back in his hand as if he could undo this all by rewinding time. As if he could drive in reverse all the way back to his shift at the prison last night and sit over a cup of crappy coffee and watch the CCTV forever, keeping his son alive indefinitely by never finding him dead in the first place.

He looked down and found his phone in his hand and his thumb hovering, his professional training moving his body calmly through a grief he found himself now, already, unable to express. Clearing the bile from his throat, he dialed 911 and delivered the nature and location of his emergency, identified himself and the deceased and weapon found, and explained that it wasn't an emergency any longer, but the medical examiner would be required. He leaned against the truck and waited. He would wonder, later, at all the detail he failed to inspect, all the things he didn't know. How he could be such a poor witness, after all these years trained and paid to watch, to notice. How shock and grief could hollow him out so totally and so quickly that he had no answers to questions a father should have known, should have wanted answers to immediately and gone looking for himself.

Every question the officers, then detectives, asked him with a professional courtesy blended with pity put a hum of white noise in his head. Every question another blow to his hollowed-out core. A pain so total that he didn't understand his mouth working, or his own hand moving across a page. Why hadn't he read the letter? Why would his son leave him such detailed instructions? Did he see his son making gift bags of his favorite belongings for each of his friends, the night before? Did he know any of those friends? What about the emails his son wrote to his siblings, what did he think they said? Why didn't any of his other kids live with him? Did his son seem depressed back then, when he made his own decision to live with his father? Did his son know about the gun, even then? Every question, what sure stuff the man was made of crumbled, until he thought he was answering questions from his knees.

Did his son know about the gun, even then?

Heather Brooks

Light and Wildflowers

Secrets kept through out the years
A wall was built from all her tears
Lost in darkness, what was real
Fully numb, she could not feel

Alone she wept to hide her pain
Hoping she'd never have to explain
That pushing deeper in the night
Is where she planned to give up her fight

She closed her heart and decided to go
How long it'd take she did not know
A spirit broken, a soul so shattered
She believed it no longer mattered

A warmth so strong against her wall
Pushing through she heard it call
Opening her eyes, it grabbed her hand
A light so bright it changed her land

The truth she felt, she could not hide
A beautiful beacon by her side
Darkness fading, no longer found
Only hope was all around

Shining bright so close above
It filled her heart with so much love
Shaping her land to be empowered
She planted herself amongst the wildflowers

Trust

A simple word with a complex meaning.
Hard to grasp and leaves me feening.

Words flowing at me like a whitewater rapid.
I'm eroding, left maladapted.

Broken promises drift down the stream
Pulling me deeper, yet I don't scream.

Lost in a sea of skepticism, don't believe
All the things people say to me.

Hoping for the day they finally unearth
The fragments of my beat up worth.

Maybe then will they set to adjust
How to handle other peoples trust.

Gwendoline Correges

The Roaches of Our Minds

It'd been a while since I'd stopped by Bill's, you know, quarantine and all. We were neighbors for years and I'd always randomly pop in and find him playing records or editing skate videos. A couple of times he cooked for me, always something vegetarian, something tasty. I've spent hours in his little kitchen, smoking cigs, bantering, sometimes outright disagreeing, but always laughing. I appreciated our friendship. Bill was a smart, colorful individual with very specific likes, dislikes and habits. You could say he was faithful to himself. It only seemed natural that, riding past his house, I would stop by and say hi. It'd been what? Four months? Five? We were due.

I parked my bike along the sidewalk and hiked though the knee high weeds. Bill was never the type to manicure a lawn but this felt a bit hectic. I passed the old rotting motorcycle that clearly hadn't moved since last time I'd been over, opened the squeaky gate to let myself into the backyard, and slid along the fence and between this busted trailer that had also, just been rotting here. When he first got the trailer I thought it was cool. I imagined Bill cruising to the beach with his dog, his bestest of best friends. He was always a minimalist and I had no trouble imagining that that trailer would hold everything he ever needed. It felt free. But now that I was seeing it again, sunken deeper into the dirt, moldier and more rusted from the rain, derelict, I got a weird feeling in my gut. The whole outside of the house reeked of severe neglect, almost like no one had been home throughout quarantine. I suddenly got the feeling that randomly stopping by like this might be totally inappropriate. But it was too late. The dog started barking and I saw Bill's head peering out the kitchen window. He came to the door in a stained, sleeveless jersey. He barely smiled. "Come in." "Is it cool? I don't wanna interrupt anything." "Nah, I'm just editing some videos." And we walked to the kitchen. I felt relieved. Everything was the same. We sat down, lit some cigarettes and started talking about the past few months. He had lost his job at the bar but was now working full time on his videos, editing, packaging, sticking stickers, mailing envelopes, and repeat. I asked him if he'd been seeing anyone. He said not so much.

I heard some rummaging behind me a few times. The third time I turned around I saw a huge cockroach walking all over the dishes. Bill looked at it and shrugged his shoulders. "Ehh." "I have an amazing product for that,"I told him. "No. I'm not going to use something toxic and make my dog sick," he retorted. Then the roach made more noise and he got up and sprayed it with a can of Raid. I was confused. He sat back down. There was an awkward silence, and so I blurted out the first thing that came to my mind "I can't believe people are opposing the defunding the police thing. So dumb!" Bill took a drag off his cigarette and said "They're doing that so they can get rid of the police altogether and move in the feds." "They're not trying to get rid of the police Bill, they're just trying to allocate some of the police department's funds to mental health care and housing. That's not…" He cut me off, laughing, "You didn't think they were gonna shut us down like this did you?" "Actually I was in LA when they said SXSW was gonna be canceled and I immediately got on a plane because I figured I could end up being stuck there indefinitely, so I definitely was aware. And my mom lives in France Bill, they started the quarantine before we… " "But I knew! I knew they would shut us down. There'll never be a live show in Austin again. You've seen what they do now." I said I doubted we would never have live music again and he repeated once more "You didn't think they were gonna shut us down like that but I knew they would. And they did. And no one believed me! And now I'm saying there won't be any more live shows in Austin and you don't believe me, but you'll see! You wanna defund the police? You'll end up with a microchip in you. And they'll track you down," he warned me, as he was checking a notification on his iPhone, his posts geo-localized. The roaches continued to make noise, I felt like the kitchen was the inside of Bill's brain. Dark, neglected, lacking human attention, crawling with something dark. I felt scared. "You said you haven't been seeing anybody?" "Nah. I don't need to go outside. Especially when they microchip us I'm never leaving my house again." He paused for a moment. "I've had a friend come by a couple times, we did a lot of coke, stayed up all night." Then I knew what it was, what I felt when I first got here, what I was feeling again now, it was mental illness. It was oozing over everything, the house, the yard, the trailer… they were no longer mere objects, they were manifestations of Bill's mind. The roaches kept him company, like the conspiracy theories in his head. They found crumbs here in there and those crumbs kept them alive: physical trauma to the head from skating and fighting, drugs, alcohol and isolation.

How many people were like Bill right now? Lost in their own dark and twisted mental labyrinths? How many conspiracies were rotting away how many brains? I looked out the kitchen window, I could see other quiet houses, and a growing sense of dread overcame me. If he would refuse to vote to allocate funds to help the weakest people in our society, if he would work against both his own self-interest and the common good, then who else? Is it possible that the city could lose that vote, that we would willingly perpetuate a fruitless cycle of heavy taxation, misallocation of funds, oppression and abuse? I left Bill's quickly and uncomfortably, I knew I probably would never see him again. What for? This wasn't my friend. This was someone else. I was horrified. My shirt got caught on the trailer as I was trying to squeeze through, I felt the roaches were crawling on me now. I had to get out of these weeds, this space. I jumped on my motorcycle and decided to take the long way home. I needed to clear my thoughts.

How could someone so secure in who they are lost touch with reality like that? Someone so specific in the way they lived. Maybe that was the essence of the problem? His rigidity. An inability to adapt and create new neural pathways? I guess that, all kinds of people fall for conspiracy theories, they are insidious. Just like the roaches: they smell food, a kernel of trash, they find a crack to slither into and they establish themselves, eating, growing; unchecked they can really prosper. A bad foundation is like a weak brain, the neglected cognitive processes lead to hindered pattern recognition. There are cracks everywhere. We live so disconnected from nature, we no longer really use those skills to survive. We don't need to pay attention to the changes in the weather, to the migration of the birds, the marking on the ground. We can just go to the grocery store to get food, any day, any time. We can exist, like Bill, in a completely a-natural way, the hunter-gatherer in us forgotten, like an old model taking up space and dust in the corner of our subconscious. Did you know that the pilgrims systematically and severely punished those who defected from their ranks to join the natives? It was the ultimate insult. According to historical records no native who lived with the pilgrims ever chose to stay with them. They found their ways unfruitful, harsh, focused on an afterlife that promised reward for all the toiling when all along the reward was right under their nose. The United States were founded by very religious people, who instead of embracing the way the natives lived and their relationship to nature, felt disdain, felt perhaps threatened by it. There was a connection to be had with the land, with nature. It wasn't a utopia, but there was balance. And nature, violent, cruel, whatever you want to call it, works in balance. We were meant to use our minds in specific ways. And now our inner-workings are in a state of disrepair, malfunctioning, grabbing at patterns that don't exist. Maybe I'll sleep outside tonight. Maybe I'll sleep outside for a couple nights.

The Amazon Stocks

It's March 2020, early quarantine, and most of what I've done is talk shit about Jeff Bezos and how much money that guy's about to make. Fast forward to September 2020, and something pops into my head. Amazon stocks. Those things must have really increased in value in the past 6 months. I check and of course… they have. Why? Why did I just sit there and talk shit? If I knew for a fact what was going to happen, why didn't I take action? I could have transformed my savings account. I'd be selling my shares right about now. I think that's how that works. I wouldn't be greedy, I really would just be selling now. But I didn't act: I thought. And the frustration I feel towards myself is really very intense. Thankfully I can go back in time and buy the goddamn stocks.

March 2020 again, I make a brokerage account and put every bit of money I have into purchasing these shares. I can't wait to quadruple my investment. I can fix the house, fix my car, take a vacation. Boom, it only took 20 minutes. I haven't run into anyone. This couldn't have gone smoother.

September 2020 again, and I'm back in my timeline. I log into the brokerage account. The shares aren't worth shit. What?! How is this even possible?? There must be an error with the website, something is wrong. After messing around for a minute… I decide to … take a look at the news? Nothing's changed right? I didn't really do anything to alter the timeline did I? Did I accidentally do something?

"After 5 weeks, Trump is still refusing to pay the ransom for Jeff Bezos: Amazon stocks continue to plummet"

You've got to be fucking kidding me. What the hell is going on? I dig into the article: "Ecoterrorists demand protection of Arctic wildlife sanctuary in exchange for Jeff Bezos.' Are they stupid? They know Trump hates him! He's not gonna give into their demands. "Without its owner, the online retail giant has rapidly succumbed to internal malfunctions." Un-fucking-believable!

March 2020 again, I can't believe this! We're all gonna be stuck inside? For how long? I can't even get a slot for grocery delivery over at Central Market. Guess I'll have to order food from Amazon too. Man that guy's about to make a ton of money. It's too hot out here, I'm gonna go back inside. As I put my hand on the door knob I see a shadow swiftly disappearing into the hallway. Oh my god. It's already starting. The break-ins, the robberies, the murdering, the civil war! I grab a pickax and quietly go inside. I follow the shadow's steps, into my bedroom… I hear a rustling. There's someone in there! I am too freaked out. I slowly backtrack hoping whoever is in there doesn't hear me. What was I thinking?? I'm at the door… I twist the knob as gently as I can. I pull the door open… It creaks and I stand totally still. I can hear the person typing on my computer. This is so incredibly creepy and horrifying. I finally walk out the door and I run over to my neighbors. They're good friends. I bang on the door. "Jeremy! Esra! Open up!!" Esra opens the door with a serious look on his face. "What's wrong?" "Someone broke into my house! They're in there right now! I don't know what to do!" Esra tells me to go inside his house, he grabs a handgun and crosses his yard over to my place. I see him going in. Nothing. He comes back out and tells me the house is empty. I run up to him and we both look through the house. "It'll be ok" he says. I think he believes me. "I think we're about to see a lot of strange behavior with all this quarantine stuff" he asserts. He hugs me and tells me I can spend the night at his house if I want to. I tell him I'm ok and stay home.

Later that night... "Yes mom!" Esra says into his cellphone, annoyed. "Yes I know! I AM being safe. I am telling you to be cautious, there is no need to panic."

Esra's mom is a recovering alcoholic. She's at the last meeting before quarantine rules go into effect. She just got off the phone with her son. "And someone broke into my son's neighbor's house today!" A lot of concerned faces are nodding at her. "You really can't be surprised" "It's only the beginning!"

There's an electrician going through the breaker box. He turns discreetly, he's listening. He's outside now, on the phone: "Ginnie, you know how we were talking about what we were talking about last night, and we thought, yeah maybe we're overreacting and we don't need to really do anything, because this is just going to unravel itself like it always does, and... yes. Things are happening. The whole country is about to go to shit. Let's do something about it. Let's really do it."

"You want to bomb an amazon warehouse?" Ginnie's cocaine eyes light up. She inhales another fat bump out of a tiny ziploc. "I gotta tell you something. When you were telling me all this stuff last night, I didn't even believe you, because like, we were high, but why should we work our asses off, all the time, and everyone else get to make money. And yeah I got fired, and some would say it's my own damn fault. But you know what? Maybe I wouldn't like coke so much if it wasn't the only thing that entertained me... and... yeah... yeah... I said yeah! I got it goddamn it. I'll see you later."

The electrician is sitting in his car with Ginnie. "Hurry up, I don't want wait all night. I swear to god don't make me come in there to get you." He's holding her arm tight and she gestures wildly to get him off of her. "I HEARD you!". She gets out of the car and slams the door. She runs up some stairs and knocks on her dealer's door.

It's 35 minutes later, Ginnie's plastered. She's sitting on the couch talking to this weird looking ginger kid. "And he says he wants to bomb an amazon warehouse! To show them! You know? We'd be like Natural Born Killers or something."

The ginger sits back. "When I worked construction, I knew a guy who worked at Bezos' mansion. He's got security like you wouldn't believe."

"Hmm" some girl is clearing her throat. She'd been sitting in the dark. Ginnie started. "I didn't even notice you here". The girl "yeah I know. You've been talking your ass off for over 30 minutes. How about you take your shit and get the fuck out of here." "You don't need to be rude" retorts Ginnie. She takes her blow and puts it in her purse. "Til next time!" She's out the door. The girl turns to the ginger "Can you put me in touch with that guy that worked at Bezos' house? I have some moral qualms I need to assuage, and I think this might be a good way to start." The ginger isn't phased. "Sure. Here's his number. Tell him we're friends. He's kind of a dumb dude though I don't know what y… " "That's perfect. I gotta go by the way. Ethan's waiting for me. And make sure to give me that good shit, I don't want the speedy garbage you gave that moron." The ginger seems offended "I would never give you that… Have I ever once given bad drugs? Even back when we were in college and you were studying wildlife rehabilitation? Well? Did I ever?" "No… no. Of course not."

Nancy Crozier

Harbored

"Kiss me and we'll go" he said
As I was welcomed back by his body
A body I once knew
His hands intwined in my hair
Hands that once held my young body
Time has moved forward
Our electricity stayed charged
"I want to pause time" he said
I showed him the aging skin on my hands
Hands that once wrote him poetry
We compared wrinkles on our faces
Faces that never changed
Thousands of nights we spent apart
But this night I cry to you and say "I just wanted you to know"
I've seen something in your eyes since Sunday
A deep well inside, with pages of apologies
Tell me you never wanted to leave
Show me the shame you had
"Kiss me and we'll go" he said

Yellow

I want to eat crackers in bed with you
Stay up as late as we can
Fall asleep with all the lights on
I want to step on wildflowers
In a field we accidentally have found
Playing hooky from our jobs
Abandoning our obligations
I want to cover your face with your birthday cake
Wreck the kitchen with our screams
I want to be loud in museums and libraries
Being shushed at every giggle and loud smile
Gross out strangers with PDA
I want to break every rule and confuse every mundane corner of this world with you
Put our names together and leave chaos in our wake

FAR AWAY

Far off are the nights
We'd fuck in your twin bed
The moon bright through your blinds
We'd sleep and fit together there somehow
I'd write messages on the mirror in your hallway
Or watch you string your guitar before your show
Young and wild adults we were
Broke and in love and oblivious to our futures
Your fearless eyes trapped my heart for that summer
I'd leave your apartment for work
You'd sleep til your next class
Who knew when you told me you loved me this whole time
We were breaking up
Or you're a thousand miles away

Thomas Deschain

10:30

It's 6am again
I wake up at the same time every morning
No sunlight
No sound besides one of the mutts snoring
Last night you told me you didn't want to be here anymore
I lay here and wonder if today is the day
What would I even do?
I'm terrified to move
Wondering how I'll find you this morning
It's like Schrodinger's cat
You exist in both life and death until I see you
I wait
And I wait
The noise of the morning comes
"I'm not going to make it through the night"
I can't help but think that today is the day you don't make it
It takes an unseen force to get me out of bed
I turn the coffee on
I let the dogs out
I find other distractions
10:30am. It's time to take your medication

Burroughs

Do people think this guy was a writer?
He reminds me of the guy screaming nonsense on the corner
"The end is nigh!"
Art for art sake
It's bullshit. It always has been
Andy Warhol was the same way
Subversive without purpose
Uncomfortable for the reaction
There's no staying power. Not really
We have lousy pedestals

Questionable Summer

"What would you do if someone handed you the winning lotto ticket?"
These are questions we start asking ourselves to get to know each other.
It's a starting point.
"What is an important item for you to carry with you at all times?"
I've got questions.
Explain to me depth.
Where is the substance? Where is the meaning?
"Would you break the law to save a loved one?"
These are real questions.
The therapist thinks this will be helpful to bridge the gaps
Instead of hollering at each other.
Tell me how you would hire your wedding singer.
Explain to me why you think orange is an important word.
How do you want to be buried?

If you even want to be buried.

Zephin Livingston

Yoos Goes for a Walk

Kayjusb the Many-Angled Tyrant was lonely. Not bored, mind you, being a polygonal despot meant having to handle a great many problems coming at it from all sides. But few of them involved interacting with its fellow sapient beings. It saw plenty of them, sure, but all they said were things like "By the gods, what *is* that thing?" or "How do we kill it?" or, occasionally, "What are you doing in my basement?" The answer to the latter question is usually "because it's nice and cool down here," though few get to hear it say this before the screaming starts.

The primary duty of Kayjusb the Many-Angled Tyrant was to be the monster in the dark. Every dark. Kid afraid of a monster under their bed? Kayjusb the Many Angled Tyrant. Group of heroes coming across a horrifying beast while delving into a dungeon? Kayjusb the Many-Angled Tyrant. The creeping anxiety that spiders crawl into your mouth as you sleep? Not Kayjusb the Many-Angled Tyrant, actually. That's just the magic of the human mind. Kayjusb the Many-Angled Tyrant didn't deal in fear. Fear just swirled around it in a vague miasma. This was all well and good when Kayjusb the Many-Angled Tyrant stayed in the dark where it belonged, and it usually didn't mind the dark. The dark was cool, and Kayjusb the Many-Angled Tyrant overheated easily.

This left it with, well, no one. Humans couldn't hold in their screams when they saw it, animals walked the other way when when it drew near, and even the other, less terrifying primordial personifications like Imagination or The Overwhelming Feeling of Joy One Gets When Laying Eyes on a Puppy ("Ned" for short) never talked to it. Even Thermodynamics was held in higher regard, and unlike Kayjusb, Thermodynamics killed people.

This was usually fine. Kayjusb could supplement its social starvation by lurking in the dark, just out of sight, and listening to the comings and goings of mortals. It watched happy couples walking hand-in-hand, childhood friends chattering amongst themselves about whatever popped into their heads, and just the general hustle and bustle that came with living in an impermanent world.

As it listened to the white noise of civilization on this day, something inside the Many-Angled Tyrant stirred, slithered, and occasionally buzzed, its gaze now fixed on one of the happy couples walking hand-in-hand, the sun blessing them with its warmth and light, the grass cushioning their footfalls, the wind keeping them cool. Thoughts began bubbling in the rusted cauldron of its mind. Why couldn't it go out into the light for once? What need was there to stay in the dark at all times? Other primordial personifications took breaks all the time, why is its situation so different? Why couldn't Kayjusb the Many-Angled Tyrant just go for a walk?

So it did.

–

This was, to put it lightly, a logistical nightmare for the Celestial Bureau for Universal Maintenance (C.B.U.M.). A god decides to descend from the heavens, that's fine. At worst, they'll get indignant, raze a village or two, maybe lay with a mortal who thinks they're just a rather fetching swan. These things were expected. But Kayjusb the Many-Angled Tyrant taking a walk was like Magnetism going on a vacation or Gravity calling a babysitter so it can have a night out on the town. The universe at large didn't really know how to go on without it. If Kayjusb the Many-Angled Tyrant wasn't in the dark, then what was?

Cyrus Crawford, Chief of C.B.U.M., was currently tearing his arm hairs out over the whole situation. The hair on his head left this world after Entropy and Imagination got married and went on honeymoon last year. Whatever was left couldn't be styled, more politely asked to part in one direction or another. The man's heavy jowls rumbled with anxiety. His assistant brought him a cup of tea to calm his nerves. Cyrus's manic eyes glared down at the mug erroneously titled "World's Best Boss." He wasn't the world's best boss! He was a terrible employer! He'd been appointed to the position of chief because his stepfather was a senior member of The Powers That Be! He didn't know the first thing about keeping a universe running; he barely knew how to turn on his computer. Science made about as much sense to him as any other foreign language, and it took him five months on the job to realize Uranus was a planet!

The only saving grace of the position was that, thankfully, Cyrus didn't have to go out and find Kayjusb the Many-Angled Tyrant himself. He had people for that.

A common prank pulled by senior C.B.U.M. agents was to convince rookies that the Bureau's *real* job is to perpetuate myths, folktales, and legends so that no one looks underneath to see what the Powers That Be are *really* doing to people's drinking water, antibiotics, or shoelaces. The rookie agents generally buy this right up until they're forced to arrest an eight-legged *kitash-ai* from Planet VK-IV who happened to be squatting in the mind of a dead-eyed night janitor. Kate Gadsen never got the joke. Even after years of negotiating with "gods," "wizards," and "time travelers," her disbelief never faltered. It was all a ruse to her, a smoke-and-mirrors show for the masses, and she was happy to be part of the show. To that end, she dressed like an alien from a bad 50s movie, all silver and shoulder pads and bleached pompadours. Her fellow agents regarded her with a mix of confusion and fear, but she wore the title of "agent" with pride.

Speaking of titles, "Rockstar" Rick Goldsmith had won a great many titles: Classic Championship Wrestling Southwestern Heavyweight Champion, C.B.U.M June 1966 Employee of the Month, Guinness World Record Holder for Longest Marathon on Space Mountain (72 hours, 16 minutes, 4 seconds). He was the very definition of the term "conmen," all easy smiles and smooth turns of phrase charms and deft sleight-of-hand. There were two ways to fool people, in Rick's eyes. One way was to be quiet, unassuming, intentionally drab. You could quietly worm your way into any situation and perform whatever roguish task you'd set out to do without anyone being the wiser. The other method was to be Rick Goldsmith, all brightly-colored, high-collared shirts with chest hair on display; loud, heavy boots; and ostentatious Stetsons covered in rhinestones. Anyone that loud and outrageous had to be a trustworthy fool. Otherwise, why would he dress like *that*? In the art of bombastic subtlety, Rick Goldsmith was a master. He was also the one who convinced Kate that the Bureau's work was all a smokescreen, a move he had regretted every day since.

The pair walked into Cyrus' office, and the door shut behind them. In order to keep the Bureau's presence on Earth a secret, the chief's office wasn't the most spacious. In fact, it was run out of the men's bathroom of a gas station in De Smet, Idaho. Rick took a seat on the toilet paper rack, resting his stetson on his knee. Kate remained standing. Cyrus wiped the sweat from his forehead with a handkerchief.

"Agent Gadsen, Agent Goldsmith—"

"Ah ah ah, Chief," Rick wagged his finger. "You'd best address us with our proper titles, our correct nomenclature, our earned distinctions."

Cyrus sighed. "Excuse me. Agent Third Class Gadsen, esquire, and CCW Hall-of-Famer Agent Second Class Goldsmith. Better?"

Rick leaned back in his chair. "'Esquire?'"

"I *did* have a life before this job."

"Yeah, but one where you're an esquire? I thought you didn't believe in time travel and such modes of temporal conveyance."

"What?"

"Shoot, do folks still have esquires these days? Must be one of them European things. I never worked Europe."

"That's not—"

"Just leave it, Agent Gadsen," Cyrus said. "You have more important things to worry about."

"What? Another 'alien' to arrest? Another crop circle to burn into the ground so a geriatric farmer can have a conniption and be put in a home? Oh, I know, another 'wizard' needs to be put under contract so he can practice his 'magic' without legal reprisal?"

"I *do* like burnin' crop circles, Chief."

"We're pretty good at it, too. The actor playing Empress Zebula said as much last time we saw her."

"Before shootin' at us."

"Showbiz types are flaky." Kate shrugged. "It happens."

"With a laser pistol."

"The rich get all the good stuff."

Cyrus nodded sagely. "Indeed we do. On the bright side, you won't have to deal with laser pistols on this next assignment."

"Which is…"

"You must track and capture Kayjusb the Many-Angled Tyrant."

Kate laughed. "Who's that? Some weird spider puppet like that guy back in March?"

Rick rose to his feet, letting his stetson fall to the tile floor. He turned to leave.

"C'mon, Katie."

"Agent Goldsmith!" Cyrus shouted after him. "Where do you think you're going?"

But Rick was already out of the bathroom. Kate apologized to her boss and followed after Rick, leaving Cyrus to sit on his porcelain throne. Rick's forgotten stetson glimmered under the fluorescent lights.

–

Not much was known about Kayjusb the Many-Angled Tyrant. Some believed it to be a gigantic, pulsating brain with legs. Others said it was a writhing mass of spiders, scorpions, snails, and similar spineless beings all slithering along, only connected by a central nervous system composed entirely of the skeletons of children who talk back to their parents. Both of these, and many others, were true, depending on your perspective. One fact about Kayjusb the Many-Angled Tyrant that *was* known, however, is that it walked. Whether or not it walked on two legs, four legs, eight thousand legs, or one leg, it walked. It did not hover or swim or roll. This can lead to some mistaking it for a human.

Kayjusb the Many-Angled Tyrant, upon deciding to leave the darkness, found itself in a broom closet. It was cramped, but not uncomfortably so. The various appliances were neatly arranged, and the thin layer of dust that covered everything tickled only one of the Tyrant's noses. On the grand scale of broom closets, it would rank quite highly.

But, Kayjusb was here to walk, not admire the alphabetical arrangement of cleaning solutions. So, with a slimy tendril grasping the handle, it opened the door and stepped out into the wide world of Rutherford B. Hayes Middle School, currently between lunch and fifth period. Really, the screams were a bit excessive. A particularly sensitive faculty member fainted into a nearby trash can. Kayjusb the Many-Angled Tyrant scratched what could be assumed to be its head.

"Sup."

The Tyrant tilted one of its eye stalks down. It was a human child. They were called humans, yes? It couldn't remember. The child blew some sort of pink substance into a bubble then let it pop.

"You're dressed weird. Want to get lunch?"

Kayjusb the Many-Angled Tyrant formed a square mouth to speak out of.

"Greetings/Salutations/Hello. Lunch sounds/appears/seems to be lovely." It paused. "You wish to eat/dine/consume with us?"

The human child arched an eyebrow and moved an errant brunette lock of hair out of their face.

"You talk weird, and your costume doesn't look right."

"This is not a costume/disguise/façade."

The human child shrugged. "Whatever gets you through Halloween, man. You got a name?"

"We/they/I am called Kayjusb the Many-Angled Tyrant." The Tyrants' feathers puffed with pride.

"That's a mouthful. Can I call you 'Yoos' instead?"

The Tyrant stroked its chitinous mandible and pondered. "This is acceptable/tolerable/admissible." Yoos paused. "What is *your* name/designation/appellation?"

"Orin."

All seventy-six of Yoos's heads nodded in unison. "That is a good/lovely/aesthetically-pleasing name."

"Thanks." Orin turned their back to the Tyrant and headed for the door. The screams had died down, and everyone simply stared. The human brain has a tendency to lock up when viewing something it shouldn't, every neuron working toward processing how exactly the body should respond. Screaming was fun and all, but at some point you had to breathe and consider giving your poor lungs a break. Kayjusb the Many-Angled Tyrant barely had a concept of what a lung was, but in the interest of politeness, said to the stunned students and terrified teachers, "Sincere apologies for scaring/frightening/horrifying you all. May the rest of your day be well/enjoyable/eminently agreeable."

Depending on where they stood, some students would swear up and down that it bowed before shuffling out the door.

Orin led the cubic mass that was now called "Yoos" out of the school and toward what Yoos assumed was a place to acquire food. The building's preference for the color yellow was a bit disconcerting to the Tyrant. It turned its eyes to the child.

"Correct/amend/repair me if I am wrong, but are you not of the age to be attending school?"

"Yup."

Yoos paused. "Then should you not be at your school/academy/educational institution?" Orin stopped. "Why have we stopped/halted/ceased movement?"

"The light's red," Orin said, pointing. There was, indeed, a red light, several in fact, forming the shape of a hand.

"Does this happen often/frequently/on a regular basis?"

"Yeah," Orin shrugged. "Traffic, you know?"

Yoos smiled. "We *do* know/notice/perceive."

Orin shot the Tyrant a look. "You don't have to keep the act up. We're out of school, you know."

"The color/pigment/shade is green. What does that mean/mark/signify?"

Orin grunted and crossed the street, Yoos followed. The stopped cars and their passengers watched Yoos and wondered aloud how anything like that could possibly move at all. Then they asked themselves why it was following a child. Then the drivers screamed because their cars were talking. The cars were amazed it took them this long to notice.

The restaurant was thinly-populated despite it being lunch time. A couple tables were occupied by lone diners. A family of four had claimed one of the booths. Yoos's wings fluttered curiously as it watched them eat. Orin elbowed the Tyrant's fleshy hip.

"Don't stare, you'll make us look like a couple of weirdos."

Yoos stared at the child.

Orin looked away. "Yeah okay, fair."

The pair looked up at the menu displayed in bright yellow font. Orin had to squint to make out the letters. Sighing, they turned to Yoos. "Do you know what you want?"

"What/How/Why is a 'Doodlicious Flurry Supreme'?"

"It's just a big milkshake. I think they dip a bunch of fries in it and put a cherry on top."

There are few concepts that are universally known. For example, someone from the planet Cerrulitus might tilt their head at the idea of a tree while the word "bacon" means "I'd very much like to murder your youngest sibling" to the people of the Makeer System, but everyone, from the smallest amoeba to sentient stars the size of our solar system, has a concept of time. Words are even harder, what with the uncountable number of languages spoken at any given point in history. What might be a lovely compliment to one person is a plural subjunctive meaning "livestock given as a marriage proposal" to another.

There is, however, one word that miraculously keeps its meaning no matter what, even in languages that don't have a word for any of its components, even on worlds where the main form of communication is blows to the head with a big stick. It survives, nay, thrives against all manner of linguistic logic.

That word is milkshake.

Yoos darted to the counter. The cashier, seeing a winged wolf-spider wearing her mother's face as a bandana, began to scream. Yoos put its least-disgusting hand on her mouth.

"Yes, I am sure/certain/confident you are very eager to get on with the screaming like every other mortal we have come across." Yoos looked down at Orin. "Except/excluding/other than them, but I have not figured out why that is. Anyway, before you resume/continue/recommence your shouting, I would like to place an order. Is/would/might that be permissible?"

The terrified cashier nodded. Yoos did its best to smile. Unfortunately, she still saw the wolf spider. So, the mouth that ended up smiling was her mother's. The cashier screamed through Yoos's hand. Its mandibles tapped together patiently, Orin played *Tetris* on their phone, and the restaurants' patrons quietly exited the building en masse.

–

The food was uneventful and the milkshake unspectacular. Orin munched quietly while Yoos consumed the milkshake in a single, vacuous slurp.

"Woah, you finished that fast."

Yoos nodded.

"Sorry I'm taking so long."

One of Yoos's heads tilted to the side quizzically. "Why/wherefore/for what reason?" "Well you're already finished."

Yoos nodded.

"And I'm not."

Nod.

"And you're just watching me eat now."

Nod.

"And that doesn't bother you?"

Yoos considered this. "Ought/must/should it?"

Orin took a sip from their drink. "Well it bothers most people I eat with."

"Who do you normally eat/dine/consume with?"

"Who do you think?"

Yoos scratched its beak with a baby-sized hand. "I am not certain/sure/positive. Could you inform/notify/tell me?"

"My family, ya dingus. Who else?" Orin flicked a french fry at the Many-Angled Tyrant. Yoos caught it with tendril and examined its salty crevices.

"Do you have a family, Yoos?"

Yoos paused.

"Once/At one time/in the past, yes."

"What happened to them?"

"I suppose they must be dead/not alive/departed."

"Oh."

"What about your family/relatives/household?"

Orin shook their head. "You don't want to hear about that."

"But I asked/inquired/requested information."

"It's a whole thing, I don't want to get into it."

Yoos nodded and returned to studying the french fry, its length, its dimensions, its sodium content. Its crispy shell was lightly yellowed. When cracked open, a fluffy white substance was revealed. Yoos hesitantly took a bite of the fry and recoiled. Much too salty.

"My mom's just been really overbearing lately."

Yoos looked up.

"My sister just moved to college, and Mom's been directing all her parenting energy in my direction since she's not around to be the primary target anymore. She just doesn't give me any space! My dad's not been much help either. He doesn't really get what's going on with me. He tries, and I love him for it, but if he invites me on one more goddamn fishing trip, I'm gonna jump into Lake Okoboji myself. I need Me Time. You know what I mean?"

Yoos nodded in agreement, understanding nothing.

"It's kind of why I left school with you. I had to get away from it all, and you with your weird costume and your weird way of talking, it felt different. I need different right now, I think." They smiled. "So thanks."

Yoos attempted to smile back, but the attempt went about as well as when it tried to smile at the cashier. Orin laughed.

The rest of the meal was conducted in silence. Yoos studied the intricacies of how chairs worked, Orin munched on their small army of chicken nuggets, the whole thing was over in five or so minutes. Fast food.

—

The pair found themselves in a park, shockingly empty for the middle of the day. A couple of squirrels darted from tree to tree. Water spewed from the mouth of a marble goose while store-bought goldfish skittered around the pond. Orin sat on a bench. Yoos, depending on the angle, stood or sat next to it. Unlike most of humanity, the sun was very happy to see the Many-Angled Tyrant and made everything obnoxiously bright.

"You gonna take that costume off?" Orin asked. They wiped sweat off their brow with their shirt. "You've gotta be steaming under all that material. My friend Billiam, his name's William but I like Billiam better, cosplays and he's always complaining about how hot his costumes are."

"I do not sweat/perspire/expel water through my skin holes. I am feeling quite warm/hot/boiling however."

Orin laughed. "Right, my bad."

Yoos watched a pigeon land on the marble goose. It stared at the Tyrant curiously. To the pigeon, all things that move are pigeons. The trees in the park were Leafy Pigeons. The humans who fed it were Handy Pigeons. Fish were Water Pigeons. This train of thought was shared by all but the most intelligent of pigeons, who knew that trees couldn't be pigeons because you can't build a nest on another pigeon. To the pigeon, Yoos seemed to be a collection of pigeons, all with their own feathers and beaks and eyes, except they all squawked in unison. Really, the pigeon was just impressed that they could coordinate so well. One of the birds making up Yoos's pigeon-body plucked at its feathers.

"What do you see/observe/espy when you look at me, Orin?"

Orin scratched their chin. "Some anime character? Not one I've seen, but it's got all those points and edges and the bony chest. Is it from an anime?"

Yoos's knee-pigeon shrugged. "That is possible/feasible/potentially true, but we do not know."

Orin looked up. "Then why the costume? It looks really hard to make. Isn't the point to dress up as a character from a thing you like?"

Yoos sat down on the bench as best it could. The problem with being many-angled was that you rarely fit in most places, at least comfortably. Sitting was particularly uncomfortable. But it was tired of being upright, and laying down seemed worse.

"This is not/has never been/will never be a costume."

"Oh come on, it's obviously a costume!" They grabbed at Yoos. A sharp pain surged up their arm. They yelped and drew their hand back and saw blood leak out of a couple fingers. "What is that *made* of?" They suckled and tasted copper. "That really hurts. Why didn't you warn me?"

Yoos looked down, concerned. "I didn't know it would hurt/harm/cause injury."

"How did you not know? Do you not know what you look like? Do you not see the spikes? I thought they were some kind of plastic."

"I don't know how I look/appear/seem to you."

There was silence.

"Is something wrong/unsettling/displeasing?"

After another silence, Yoos continued, "I don't know/possess information about/have awareness of how I appear to anyone. I never have/never did/never will. Everyone/anybody/all people see me differently. When I look/view/observe myself in a mirror, I see nothing. So I did not know about the spikes/prongs/barbs. I am sorry/regretful/shamefaced that they hurt you." It paused. "I enjoyed/liked/relished meeting you, Orin. It was short/brief/relatively uneventful, but pleasant. Thank you."

Yoos did its best to smile again. Orin, finally understanding what Yoos *was*, did what everyone else did, screamed, and ran off. Yoos sat alone. Occasionally, a curious pigeon hopped forward to see what all the fuss was about regarding this pigeon hivemind but promptly lost interest after realizing the collective wasn't sharing any food.

-

After enough pep talks to empower several major sports leagues and sufficient alcohol to knock out André the Giant, Agents Kate Gadsen and "Rockstar" Rick Goldsmith approached Kayjusb the Many-Angled Tyrant. Whatever horrors they saw, there were now two of them. In Rick's mind, the whole thing was just another stop on the loop, another tag team match. Gadsen would start off strong only to get beaten down by the sheer horror of the Tyrant. Eventually, after struggling and grasping for freedom, she'd make the hot tag, and the Rockstar would run wild on it. A big boot, a lariat, a 1-2-3, and they'd celebrate with more brewskis at this dive bar that doesn't ask questions as long as your money's good and your liver's strong. In Kate's mind, she'd already skipped to the part where she could drink more booze.

"Alright, Mr. Tyrant, we're C.B.U.M. Agents, and we need you to come back to the Dark, alright? We don't want any trouble."

The Tyrant's gaze flitted between the two. It stood, the agents stumbled backwards. Rick tripped over one of the curious pigeons.

"Why/Wherefore/For what reason?"

"I'm sorry?"

"I want/desire/would like to know why you wish me to leave."

"Well, we'd rather you get back to where you belong... sir? Is it a 'sir'? Are you a sir? Wow, you're blurry. What are you—"

Rick tagged in and clasped a hand over his partner's mouth. "Apologies, Your Majesty, she's a chatty drunk. We'd really prefer if you moved on out of here though. You scare folks, and don't you got a home to go back to?"

"I have spent/consumed/expended enough time in the Dark, Agents. There is nothing/nil/nada there. No being/person/sentient existence besides my own." It whipped its shoulder tendrils with an appropriate amount of menace. "You mortal/finite/small people fear me now, but I think/hope/believe that if I stay, this will not always be the case. Am I not allowed/permitted/authorized to experience the joys you experience daily?"

Sweat poured off Rick like he'd just finished a 60-minute broadway with Dusty at the Omni. He swallowed, opened his mouth to speak, but Kate shoved him aside.

"Wanna get a drink?" she asked.

Yoos and Rick stared.

"What? You want to experience the things we 'small people' get to enjoy every day right?"

One of its lupine heads nodded.

"Great. I do too. Let's go!"

"Katie, we can't take him drinkin', he'll give the whole bar a damn heart attack!"

"More for us then. Let's get going, Mr. Tyrantman."

The incredibly inebriated Agent Gadsen stumbled off in the vague direction of alcohol. The newly-christened Mr. Tyrantman followed behind. Agent Goldsmith gawked for a time before running off after them.

–

Roy's Bar and Grill was less a restaurant and more a three-part trial for the senses. Upon entering the establishment, your nose would be bombarded with a cacophony of smells, some of which humanity had yet to even name. If you could weather that olfactory onslaught, your stomach would be tested next by the grease-filled concoctions which were theoretically food but were in practice low-grade bioweapons conducting a concentrated campaign on your digestive system. Finally, there was the booze so dangerous that asking a heavyweight boxer to repeatedly strike your liver for ten minutes straight would be less damaging.

Naturally, it was Katie's favorite bar in town, a fact that confounded Rick more than Katie's complete disbelief in the supernatural and extraterrestrial. Rick himself could manage the smell just fine but usually threw the food on the ground. Its grey/green coloring complemented the theoretically-clean floors quite nicely. But the drinks were shockingly tasty for the first three sips before his tongue went numb. Yoos, though unfazed by the near-toxic atmosphere, found the heat a little much and requested a drink with many ice cubes for its hand-tendrils to quietly suckle on.

The day dragged on. Rick passed out after his second glass of what was *called* a "Blue Moon Screwdriver" but looked and glowed more like something used to power starships in the
Hockey Stick Galaxies, Kate continued downing beverages with a ferocity unmatched in three solar systems, and Yoos watched. It occasionally took a sip of its beverage, exchanged pleasantries with Kate and the thin bartender Georg, but mostly it watched. As the sun fell, more patrons filed into the small establishment. These patrons barely paid Yoos any mind as they drank and talked about their lives in what was a regular ritual for most of them. Yoos listened as they explained how their bosses were jackasses, how their family didn't appreciate them enough, how they didn't appreciate themselves enough. This was not entirely dissimilar from what Yoos did while in The Dark, but this time, if anyone looked at it, there were no screams, no attempts to light it on fire, no great cries of "Monster!" Yoos felt a comfortable warmth in one of its presumably

vestigial organs. Whatever miasma of fear that circulated it seemed to be an afterthought at best on this night.

Eventually, however, even these patrons left the bar. Georg asked Kate to pay and drag Rick's sleeping carcass out into the fresh air once more. Yoos followed behind, carrying Rick's legs in its mandibles.

Kate turned to the Many-Angled Tyrant and, dizzily, said "Wow, I don't think I've met anyone who could last a whole night in that bar 'sides me. You're pretty cool, Mr. Tyrant, all three of ya."

"I am pleased/gratified/thankful for the compliment, Agent Gadsen. This day/span of time/solar rotation was better than I could have hoped."

"Ohhhh I'm glad to hear it!" She pulled Rick up over her shoulders to properly carry him. "Anyway, I gotta sleep off this hangover, and if I don't get him home by 2:30 am, Rick *will* puke on the sidewalk, and he hates doing that."

The Many-Angled Tyrant opened one of its jagged, toothy mouths to protest, to assure the agent that it would not be a bother at all. It could help carry the plastered cowboy, perhaps. It could even help the pair on their cases for the C.B.U.M. It would make itself useful, just don't ask it to go back to the Dark. All these thoughts rushed through the sinews of its mind, sprinting to a mouth to be spoken, to be freed out into the world as Yoos was itself.

But Agent Gadsen wasn't finished.

"And hey, you come back sometime, alright? I could use a better drinking buddy than this sack of rhinestones," she said, motioning to Rick.

It paused. "Come back," she said. An invitation. Kayjusb the Many-Angled Tyrant never received invitations. Its mind flashed back to the bar with its gregarious patrons and odd smells. It could return, one day, when the stars aligned.

"I think/believe/expect I will accept that offer," it said, contorting its malformed features into a half-smile-half-grimace. "I desire/wish/hope for your continued health and happiness." It turned its gaze upward, away from the agent and her unconscious companion and toward the
twinkling night sky. Toward the Dark. Toward home. "So long/farewell/goodbye."

And with that, the Tyrant walked away. It passed the agents, the bar, the state, the planet, the galaxy, turned left at Andromeda, and found the small door to its home.

With a click and a turn, Kayjusb the Many-Angled Tyrant was back where it belonged, alone with its thoughts and the Dark. For now.

Ocean Song

As the cab speeds off, you hope you left the driver a good tip. You'd never had to tip anyone yourself before; your parents handled that and, since the beginning, had drilled it into your head that tipping was incredibly important and necessary and that one should always tip a good amount. The rectangular club dominates your field of vision. It's not a terribly big building, not even as big as your house or your school-- at least those places have a second floor, but your house also has your parents, your school has your classmates and teachers. This club, for you, has nobody. A pair of women slip past you while you gawk, then another, then a trio. After about the fifth or sixth group passes, you grip your purse, straighten your back and march in.

The club soon dispels this determination. The people are loud; the smell of smuggled, cheap vodka intermixed with what you think might be cigarettes invades your lungs; and the venue is packed to the gills with people, mostly women, all talking about bands that you'd never heard of. Various glass bottles are passed around out of sight of the club staff. You manage to find some space on a wall. People do come up to you and make brief conversations about the weather ("So fucking hot!"), the show ("When is it going to fucking start?"), and the *Silence of the Lambs* ("fucking rad!"). You had never heard anyone swear that much, not even your father when the Supersonics were losing, and the size of the venue and the volume of the crowd meant that any conversation required getting nose-to-nose with whomever you were speaking to. Still, the talks comfort you. Your back slouches a bit, and your shoulders relax. The feeling that you might not belong in this cramped, cool world doesn't really kick in until a flannel-cocooned girl with sea green hair grabs you by the shoulder and, slurring, shouts, "Hey, Choir Girl! How was church service?"

She is, of course, talking about your clothes, the yellow sundress with black polka dots that clings to your still-in-that-awkward-phase body and the cloche hiding the messy bundle of strands you call your hair. Combined with the horn-rimmed glasses and tiny purse on your shoulder, your outfit makes you look like someone's moderately-fun aunt who never stops talking about her gardening. You blush and stammer out what you think might be a clever reply but actually comes out as a series of stutters and half-words. Green Flannel Girl laughs. You grip your elbows and bite the inside of your cheek until you taste copper. The pain doesn't relax you as much as you'd like and you wonder why you thought it would be a good idea to come to this concert in the first place.

You first heard about the concert during 4th period. Mrs. Doctorow was talking about the historical significance of the invention of sliced bread — her grandfather often played cribbage with the man who invented it which you're told is very exciting. You were in the middle row, not too noticeable but not too obscure, bravely battling the oncoming tide of sleepiness that often occurred when Mrs. Doctorow opened her mouth when the whispered words "Bikini Kill" caught your ears from the back row. You knew what those words meant individually but didn't know quite how they belonged together. So, you casually leaned back in your desk and listened closer. You could only catch snippets in-between your teacher's droning, but you got three key pieces of information: "Bikini Kill" was the name of a punk rock band, they were playing an all-ages show next Wednesday, and said show was being held at the North Shore Surf Club.

You knew nothing about this band, but you were intrigued. You had only recently discovered, with the help of the *Cinema Paradiso* soundtrack, that music could make you feel things, and you wanted to see what other kinds of music could make you feel things. You'd heard music before obviously, but it'd never really caught your ear. Plus, you'd never been to a concert before. So, you resolved to go. Your parents were, of course, horrified.

"Kimberly, you're only fifteen!" said your mother.

"We'd be worried sick," said your father. "And we'd have no way of making sure you're okay!"

"Exactly! Are we supposed to just call the venue? Does this 'North Surf Club' or whatever even have a phone?"

After an uncomfortably long silence, you admitted you had no idea.

"At least get one of your friends to go," suggested Mom.

"What about Marcy?" asked Dad.

You bit into your cheek and didn't have the heart to tell them that you and Marcy hadn't spoken in over two months, not since she threw a glass of milk into your face as part of a ridiculous initiation into your school's "cool clique." You told your mother and father that Marcy was busy. You told them all of your other friends were busy too. It was, after all, easy to say someone was busy when they didn't exist.

On the day of the concert, your parents were galled by your choice of clothing and sat you down in their living room with the white couch with pink polka dots to tell you this.

"You can't go out alone dressed like that!" Mom said. "If you're going, at least cover up a bit. For me."

"What if someone spills beer on the dress? That thing wasn't cheap," Dad said. He looked over at Mom who nodded. "I didn't buy that dress so you could galavant at some rock concert with a bunch of losers and dead-ends. If you mess it up, what'll you wear to the company dinner next week? Are you *trying* to embarass me?"

Thanks, Dad. He always knew to say just the right thing to make you feel like a doll but not in a "perfect Barbie doll" kind of way but in a "I am trapped in a box and can never leave that box" way. It made you feel small. But it also made you want to go to the concert more than ever. So, in your first act of teenage rebellion, you and your yellow polka dot dress snuck out, called a taxi from a payphone, and sped off to a new world of green-haired girls and cramped clubs.

Green Flannel Girl has stopped laughing at you and is instead resting her chin on your shoulder and circling the brim of your hat with her finger. You hear her say, "I'm sorry I get giggly and feely when I'm tipsy."

You stare at her for a while, chewing on your cheek. Life in the tiny club continues to move in a chaotic blur. Her eyes match her hair, you notice, and, for a brief moment, you think that she might have just been born with that hair because it looks so *right*. She's looking up at you from your shoulder with her small eyes and slight grin, expecting a reply that you've yet to give her because you're too busy counting the freckles on her cheeks. You pat her on the head twice and decide to try to use your words again. "Me too."

Green Flannel Girl-- god, you need to learn her name-- looks up at you, briefly confused. When she laughs, you laugh with her. It's stupid and unnecessary and makes you feel like a total airhead, but you keep going until you feel like your lungs are about to give out. No one in the club notices, and you take comfort in that.

Green Flannel Girl lifts her chin off your shoulder and leans onto a small patch of wall next to yours. "So what brings a girl like you to a shit club like this?"

"I just wanted to see what it was like."

"Wanted to see what?"

"You know, a concert."

"Oh!" Green Flannel Girl slaps your shoulder, the same one she grabbed earlier. It stings a bit, and you bite your cheek to push the pain down. "Well, you've come to the right woman. Stick with me, and you'll have the best night of your life."

Her grin is wide, toothy, and disarmingly pretty. Her cheeks puff out when she smiles. Her eyes scrunch up as if to give her mouth more room to smile. You start counting her freckles again. She snaps her fingers a couple times to get your attention.

"Hey, are you alright?"

"I'm fine," you say, still counting freckles.

"Are you always this talkative?"

"No, I'm usually quieter."

"Why's that?"

You shrug and stare at your shoes. Green Flannel Girl tsks and sticks her face into your field of view.

"Are you talkative enough to tell me your name?"

You pause, and before you can say anything else, the already-dim lights shut off completely except for the ones illuminating the stage. You look to the stage, and there they are:

Bikini Kill. You don't know why you expected them to wear bikinis on-stage, but you did. That they don't is throwing you through a loop. You also didn't expect a band with a name like that to have a male guitarist, but there he is, tapping his pick on his guitar. The bassist with her white dress and short blonde hair has her back to the audience and seems to be chatting with the drummer, whose hair is also cut short. Green Flannel Girl begins elbowing her way to the front of the crowd, but you don't follow. Then, the lead singer steps to the mic, guitar slung over her shoulder, hair tied up a lot like yours, center-stage. She grabs the mic with both hands and screams, "We're Bikini Kill, and we want revolution! Girl style now!"

Before you can even begin to process what she just said, you are bombarded with noise, sludgy guitar, pounding drum, a much uglier sound than the *Cinema Paradiso* soundtrack. Every lyric coming from the lead singer's mouth is dripping with unapologetic venom. Her anger is raw and unpolished, like the music, and you'd never heard someone mention cum in a song before.

Each verse shoots through you like a lightning bolt. You feel it in your fingernails. Your heart thumps in time with the drums. You're drawn in. In fact, you slip to the front row and somehow find yourselves next to one of your classmates who, if they do notice you, doesn't react. This isn't music to really dance to, but everyone is trying their best, and, eventually, you try too. After every song, the audience screams and claps and begs for more, and you add your voice to the chorus. You don't want it to stop, but eventually, it does. With a loud, "Good night!" Bikini Kill leaves, and the next band begins setting up. All you want is an encore.

"Choir Girl!" Green Flannel Girl drapes herself over your shoulder, grinning. "You really got into it, dude! That's rad."

She ruffles your hair, and you realize, with horror, that you lost your hat during the set. Your awful, stringy hair falls on your shoulders, and that makes you feel like you have ants crawling inside your blood vessels, but you collect yourself and decide to handle this unfortunate event in the sanest, most rational way possible: you bolt right out of the club and onto the streets of Olympia.

It only takes you a minute of running to realize that you might have overreacted, but you're also fairly certain that returning to the club would cause you to spontaneously combust out of embarrassment. Thankfully, hailing a taxi isn't too difficult, and you make it home without further incident.

When you step through the back door to the kitchen of your tiny house, you are greeted by the sight of your mother at the dinner table, her black bathrobe with the white polka dots slightly open, sipping what you assume is her favorite blend of Earl Grey from her "World's Best Mom" mug which she bought for herself. You put your head down and try to shuffle to your room.

"Do you have any idea how hard it was to be your mother tonight?" You stop and look at her. "What are you--"

"When you told me you wanted to go to this concert, I was worried someone would just pick you up and whisk you away to God knows where, and that would be the last I ever heard from my baby girl." Her grip on the mug tightens. "Your father and I tried to talk some sense into you, but you just couldn't resist, could you?" She takes a sip from her mug and slams it onto the table so hard you flinch. "We've spent the past three hours looking everywhere for you, you know. Your father is *still* out there looking for you. Did you once consider how we felt? You should have just listened to us to give us peace of mind, just this once. We might have let you go to the next one!"

"I told you where I was going, Mom."

Your mother explodes out of her chair and gets right in your face. She's shorter than you and shares your awful, stringy hair. Her big, green eyes are bloodshot, and her small, tight face is ruddy. "And how were we supposed to find this place, Kimberly? Do you think we just keep maps around with all the new and hot places for teens to go and waste their lives? As a matter of fact, how did *you*?"

"I asked the cab driver to take me there."

"How do you know where to find a taxi service?"

You shrug. "It's in the phone book."

A mixture of confusion, exasperation, and the realization of her and your father's collective stupidity wash over your mother's face. She backs away from you and rubs the bridge of her nose with a sigh. "Just-- just go to bed, Kimberly. It's a school night."

You don't feel tired-- you actually feel great despite the verbal lashing you just received-- but she was right about the school night thing. The last time you were late to school, you hid in your room, and the idea of eating anything made you feel physically ill. Being on-time is much healthier. So, you shuffle to your room as ordered, change into your pajamas, and flop into bed.

But you can't sleep, not even a little bit. You replay the concert in your head over and over. Your body buzzes with energy with each remembered note. In your quest to find music that made you feel things, you'd found a band that made you feel a lot of things. Then your mind wanders to Green Flannel Girl, and you wonder if she made it home okay. You wonder who she was. You wonder why her laugh was so contagious. When sleep finally takes you, all you can see is her hair, her eyes, her smile.

The next day, you're still buzzing. On the drive to school, your father tries and fails multiple times to bring up last night, tries to scold you as your mother had done. Eventually, he manages to ask, "So you talked to your mother last night?"

You nod, watching the sunny streets of Olympia speed by in a blur. In the back of your mind, you're looking for Green Flannel Girl, as ridiculous as it would be to just find her on the sidewalk or in traffic. Part of you is also looking for members of Bikini Kill, the singer with hair like yours, the faceless bassist, the short-haired drummer, the surprisingly-male guitarist, but the idea of finding *them* in traffic is even more ridiculous. They were probably already on their way to the next gig, and what would you even do if you saw one of the band or Green Flannel Girl? Would you smile and wave? Would you immediately hop out of the car, run over, and tell them how great a time you had at the concert? Would you ask them if they'd found a little black cloche on the floor last night?

Your father sighs, loudly. You look over at him. The bags under his eyes are prominent, and he's practically slumped over the steering wheel, barely controlling the car as it cruises down the street. The usual frown on your father's face is more pronounced than it normally is. You stare up at your father and, biting the inside of your cheek, ask, "Are you okay?"

"I was out there until five in the morning looking for you. Five hours! I've barely slept, and you won't even talk to me when I ask you a simple question. Did you or did you not talk to your mother last night?"

"I did."

Your father pushes up his glasses and rubs his eyes in exasperation and exhaustion. The light turns green, and you're back on your way to school.

"Okay, good. What did she say?"

"She told me how hard it is to be my mother."

Your father sighs and says, "Ain't that the truth." He looks over at you, sees your hurt expression, and reaches out with a hand to comfort you. "Hey, I didn't mean it like that, kiddo."

You move away from his touch and continue looking out the window. "No, it's okay. I understand."

You don't actually understand; you think, recent attempt at teenage rebellion aside, that you've done a pretty good job being a daughter. You don't get into much trouble, you keep your grades respectable, you help out around the house when you're needed. You're not perfect, but who is? "Difficult" would not have been the word you'd use to describe yourself. You hide behind your beanie as best you can. Your father thinks you understand and, putting his hand back on the steering wheel, says, "Well, I hope you can do better next time."

You wonder what he means by "next time," but you can't think about it too much before he's parked in the school lot, and saying, "Have a good day. We'll talk about your punishment when you get home."

You spend your school day desperately clutching your backpack as you drift from class to class. You catch the classmate who also went to the concert stealing glances at you on occasion, but he waits until after school to talk to you. He comes toward you with a smile which you find mildly intimidating because of the six-or-seven inches he has on you.

"That was *you* I saw last night, right?"

You grip your backpack just a bit tighter and nod. Your classmate snaps his finger and says, "So that *was* you I saw with Betsy." Your classmate sees the surprise painted on your face and arches an eyebrow. "Wait, you really didn't know her name? You guys seemed pretty friendly."

"She called me 'Choir Girl.'"

Your classmate laughs and says, "Yeah that sounds like her. Did you enjoy the concert?" Your grip on your backpack loosens as you begin to gush about the concert. "It was the greatest thing I've ever been to! The atmosphere was so... intimate, and the people seemed really cool, and it was-- it was kind of scary at first but I got used to it, and Betsy was really nice to me, and the music, dude, the music was so good! I'd never heard anything like that before. The songs are still buzzing in my head! Oh my god, it was the best!"

Your classmate gawks at you. You scratch the back of your head and ask, "Is everything alright?"

"Yeah no, everything's fine. Um, I think I have a cassette with some Bikini Kill on it. It's got a bunch of other bands on it too. Do you want to borrow it?"

"That'd be great!"

"Okay cool. Also, if you wanted to find Betsy again, I know there's a Melvins show coming up in, like, two days. We could maybe go and see if she's there?"

"Um, sure."

Your classmates claps his hands together and shouts, "Great! I can give you a ride home afterward."

"Cool." You pause. "I'll have to sneak out again."

"Same here." Your classmate laughs. "I don't know many parents who actually let their kids go to these concerts."

You nod. "That's comforting to know. See you there."

"Yeah, you too, Kimberly!"

He turns to walks away, but you say, "Wait!" He turns around, smiling.

"Yeah?"

You bite your cheek and fidget with your fingers a bit before asking, "Sorry but what's-- what's your name again?"

You'd never seen the light fade from someone's eyes so fast before. He stares down at the floor, shoulders slumped, even his long, black hair seems to lose some of its shine. Whatever happiness existed inside of him is fleeing at lightspeed.

"David." He turns to shamble away, a shell of his former self. "I hope you like The Melvins."

You did not like The Melvins. It probably didn't help that you spent the entire concert scanning the crowd for a hint of green hair. You dipped out during the second song of the set and went home. David was nice enough to dip out with you and give you the cassette he promised. He still looked utterly defeated the entire time though, and you wanted to say something to make him feel better but couldn't come up with anything besides a sort-of cheery "See you at school tomorrow." Unfortunately, your skills at sneaking into your house have not improved, and when you return home, your mother and father are waiting for you in the kitchen, your mother once again gripping the "World's Best Mom" mug tightly. Your father is chewing on a stalk of asparagus which he often did when he was particularly agitated. They are wearing matching blue bathrobes with black polka dots. Your mother speaks first.
"Care to explain where you were?"

"A concert."

"Did you enjoy yourself?" your father asks.

"Not really."

Your parents exchange a glance. Your father has eaten through half the asparagus. "Did something happen?" Your mother puts down the mug and inspects you for bruises, marks, anything. "Are you okay?" She grips your shoulders and looks you dead in the eye. "Did someone hurt you?"

"You can talk to us," your father says.

You shrug off your mother's frantic grabbing and back away. "No, I'm fine. It just wasn't that good of a show." And there was a distinct lack of pretty, freckled girls with green hair and wide smiles, but you weren't about to mention that part to them.

Your father finishes his asparagus.

"This needs to stop."

You nod your head and attempt to walk past them. You bump into your mother and spill a bit of her Earl Grey onto your t-shirt (you learned your lesson about how to dress for concerts).

"We're serious," she says.

"I know," you reply.

"You're going to stop?"

"I'll ask next time, I'm sorry. Can I just go to bed?"

Your mother sighs and points toward your room.

"One day you'll learn that you have to talk to your parents, Kimberly."

"Yes, ma'am." You shut your door and sit on your bed. Your body isn't buzzing like the Bikini Kill concert, and The Melvins didn't leave enough of an impression for their songs to run through your head. You can't sleep, and you feel unbearably hot so you open a window to let the wind cool you off a bit. You take out the cassette and put it into the player your aunt had gotten you when you turned seven and hadn't used since you were nine. The cassette is a compilation album, which means there is only one Bikini Kill song, but the rest of the bands made up for that disappointment by being awesome, even the Melvins who have more energy on the track than they did in-concert. Like Bikini Kill, they are all unpolished and raw, almost amateurish in some places. Some of them sound like they just picked up their instrument that same day, but some of their lyrics hit you right in the gut, and if you were afraid of your parents hearing your music, you don't care anymore. Just like the concert, you lose yourself. After the cassette ends, you flop onto your bed, huffing.

"You really get into it, Choir Girl."

Your eyes snap to the window, and there she is, leaning on the sill, green hair, green eyes, freckles. The flannel has been replaced by a green cargo jacket, and a black backpack is slung over her shoulder. You sit up, mouth agape. Betsy laughs.

"Surprised to see me?"

"Yes. How did you--"

"I saw you leaving and decided to follow you. You were with that David guy from... Olympia High? He's from Olympia High, right? That where you from?"

You nod. Betsy nods in return.

"Ok I'm not going insane. I go to Avanti High."

"I know." You pause. "It's kind of creepy that you're here."

Betsy cocks her head to the side. "What, you don't get visits from strange girls at odd hours of the night?"

"No."

"Yeah sorry. Won't happen again."

She grins. You shake your head, smile, and motion her inside. She takes a seat on the bed next to you. "So this is your palace." Betsy's gaze lingers on your *Breakfast Club*. And your *Sixteen Candles* poster. And your *Weird Science* poster, all right next to each other. "Big John Hughes fan? My grandma loves him."

"My dad used to work at a movie theatre, and he'd randomly bring me home posters." Betsy shoots you an incredulous look. You blush and look away.

"Okay, I asked him to bring me home those posters specifically."

You turn and look at her again. She wears a smug grin on her face.

"Are there any directors you like?"

"Hm…" she says, rubbing her chin. "I'm not much of a movie gal."

"Cartoons?"

"Yes!"

"Which ones?"

"Ooh, *Thundercats*. Definitely *Thundercats*. And *Scooby-Doo*. I like the ones with animals."

"That's a lot of them."

Betsy laughs and shrugs. "I like animals, what can I say?"
"Favorite animal?"

"That's like asking you to pick your favorite John Hughes movie."

"*Pretty in Pink*. Your turn."

Betsy hems and haws and flops onto the bed. She covers her face with one of your pillows, groaning.

"I don't wanna answer.

You snatch the pillow off her face and sit on it.

"I answered *your* question."

"But your question was easy!" she whines.

"Fine. Favorite kind of animal?"
Betsy sits up.

"What do you mean by 'kind'? Mammals? Birds? Vertebrates? Invertebrates? Dogs? Cats? What is this 'kind' you speak of?"

You tap your chin and make loud, pronounced "hmmmm" noises that elicit snickers from Betsy.

"Vertebrates or invertebrates?" you ask.

"Invertebrates."

"What kind of invertebrates?"

"Snails."

"Really? Why?"

"I just love the slimy little guys."

You hand Betsy the pillow which she uses to again cover her face.

"But why?" you ask.

She hems and haws, tosses and turns, does everything but answer your question. You shake your head.

"Wanna listen to the tape again?" she asks.

"I'd love to after you answer my question."

"Fine, they remind me of my grandma. They can't hear, and my grandma can't hear anymore, and so when I see a snail, I think about my grandma. That's why I like them."

Betsy covers her face with the pillow and mumbles something inaudible. You cock your head to the side.

"What?"

"I said, 'when's it gonna be my turn to ask questions again?"

You cross your arms and smile. "Go ahead."

"Why do you always cover your hair?"

You immediately grip your beanie and pull it further over your head.

"No thank you."

"No seriously, why?"

"It looks terrible."

"It didn't look that bad to me."

"You don't have to live with it. You get your perfect green hair that's all smooth and nice-looking." You tug on a small bit of hair peeking out from under your beanie. "And I get this stringy mess."

Betsy smiles. "You think my hair's perfect?"

"That's what you got from that?"

"I mean, I agree with you. It's pretty rad." She twirls a lock of her hair. "But it's nice to hear from someone else." She looks at you. "But I think your hair looks pretty rad too."

Your cheeks feel warm. You tug on your beanie. "Why did you leave the concert to follow me?" you ask.

Betsy slaps her forehead and sits up.

"Shit, right!" She opens her backpack and pulls out your cloche. It's been through a lot since you last saw it. It's wrinkled, covered in footprints, and you think you see a hole in it. "Here ya go."

You take the cloche and stare at it. You didn't hold any special attachment to the hat other than it covering your awful hair like all your other hats, and you knew you couldn't wear it in public again without mending and a long trip in the washer, but you put it on your head anyway.

"How do I look?"
Betsy laughs, loud and hard, and you with her. A little too hard, it turns out, as your father is banging on your door, shouting, "Kimberly? Who's there? Open the door!"

You respond, "I'm fine! I was just reading something funny!" You very frantically open your closet door and try to drag Betsy inside.

"A lesbian in the closet," she remarks. "Good call, Kimberly."

You stop.

"A what?"

"Is that a problem?"

"No no, I'm--"

At this moment, your dad manages to open the door, sees you with your hands on Betsy, and just stares. You slowly take your hands off her, and the three of you stand in silence. Your father sticks his hands in his pockets, Betsy plays with the collection of wristbands on her left arm, you try to look anywhere but at your father or Betsy. After a time, your mother walks in and joins the sphere of awkwardness. There is more silence.

And silence.

And silence. The leaves of the oak in your backyard rustle with the wind.

And silence.

And silence.

And silence.

Jesus, how long will it take for someone to say anything? Your feet are starting to ache from standing.

Your father leaves the room and returns with tea, in polka-dotted mugs, for everyone. Oolong. The sounds of sipping and refreshed sighs fill the space. The refreshment spurs your mother to break the silence.

"Would you mind explaining why you're in our daughter's room?"
"And why you were... you know," your father makes clumsy grabbing motions with his hands. "Doing that."

Your face flushes red. Betsy sets her mug down and puffs herself up a bit. She stands taller than your father who has never been a tall man. When she approaches him, he backs away slightly. She sticks her hand out.

"Betsy Dryden. I just dropped by to give your daughter her hat back. She lost it at the concert a couple days ago."

Your father shakes her hand.

"George Morris." He pushes up his glasses. "And the--"

Betsy stops him before he can make those grabbing motions which you appreciate. You don't think anyone wanted your father to do that again.

"We were laughing, and I fell when you started banging on the door. She was helping me off the floor."

Your father rubs his chin, nodding. Your mother looks over at you.

"Is this the truth, Kimberly? All of it?"

You freeze and try to look anywhere but at your mother.

"Well?" your mother insists.

You say nothing. Your mind is devoid of words, any words. You probably couldn't say your own name if you had to. Your mouth is dry, your throat is scratchy, and there's a dull, throbbing pain right behind your eyes. Your father crosses his arms and turns his gaze to you.

"Talk to us," he says. You don't respond. He takes a sip of his tea. "Of course not. Why would you change your behavior now? You never talk to anyone."

You bite the inside of your cheek, hard. The familiar taste of copper rests on your tongue. It comforts you a bit but not enough for you to actually say anything. Betsy is staring at you. You try to give her a smile, a nod, something to let her know that everything was fine, that you were fine.

Either you don't know how to give reassuring smiles, or Betsy saw right through your facade because she almost immediately says, "She was trying to hide me, okay? She was worried you guys would be mad at her because I showed up out of the blue and didn't want to get in trouble. Like I said, I was just giving her the hat back, and she didn't know I was coming."

Your father nods, rubbing his chin. "That makes more sense. I'm convinced. What do you think, Lorraine?"

Your mother glares at Betsy but says nothing. Another awkward silence begins to overtake the room, but you suddenly remember how to speak.

"It's almost midnight."

Your mother downs the rest of her tea and sets the mug on the floor.

"She's right. George, take Betsy home."

Your father begins to protest, but his resistance fades when your mother glances at him. He gathers everyone's mugs and motions for Betsy to follow him out the door, which she does. Before she passes the threshold, Betsy looks you in the eyes one last time and says, "I'll see you later, Kim."

Kim. No one had ever called you "Kim" before, always "Kimberly" or "Kimmy" or, when you and Marcy still talked, "Kimbo." You aren't quite sure how to feel about it, but you don't mind it as much as other shortenings of your name. There were certainly worse things to be called. Your mother visibly bristles at the nickname. When your father closes the door behind him, she says, "I take it she's the reason you've been sneaking out to these concerts."

You shake your head. Liar.

Your mother scoffs. "She's not? Oh, so you're just suddenly a fan of this… this… what sort of music is it even?"

"Punk rock."

"Oh, it's punk rock." Your mother crosses her arms and sneers. "Not only is my daughter likely never going to give me grandchildren, she also has terrible taste in music. Just perfect. Are there any other ways you'd like to disappoint me tonight?"

Your cheeks flush.

"How did--"

"Parents know their children, Kimberly."

You sigh and let your shoulders slump. You're not overly upset your mother knows-- you didn't try to hide your interest in girls-- but you had hoped she would be more accepting than this.

"How long have you known this about yourself?" your mother snarls.

"A couple years now."

"And you just kept it from us? Why? Were you afraid."

You shake your head.

"No."

"Were you ashamed?"

"No."

Your mother stands, grabs you by your elbows, keeps you rooted in place. "Then why?"

"I just didn't think it was worth mentioning."

"You didn't think the fact that you're a lesbian was worth mentioning?"

You look down. "I know how hard it is to be my parent. I know you think I should talk more. But what would you have done if I told you?"

Your mother says nothing. You chuckle.

"You would have done exactly what you did tonight: call me a disappointment." You bite the inside of your cheek and taste copper. "Do you know what's strange?"

"What?"

"You called me a disappointment, and I didn't care. I felt nothing." You look at your mother. "I think I'm going to keep going to these shows."

"And seeing Betsy?"

"And seeing Betsy."

Your mother shakes her head. "I don't think those shows are good for you."

"At the show where I met Betsy, the singer sang something. It's been playing in my head over and over again for the last two days. Do you want to know what she sang?"

Your mother says nothing. You smile.

"'If I were dead you would love me more.

Then--'" "You think I want you dead?"

"You didn't let me finish. 'Then all my words would become like gold. The angels you created would swarm my grave and lie about the way we really live.'"

"I don't understand."

"I think you want me to be something I never was."

"And what are you?"

You shrug. "I don't know. But I don't think listening to you will help me find out."

Your mother looks up at you, shocked. She stares at you; you stare back. Neither of you move. You hear the sound of your father's car pulling out of the driveway. Then, she lets go of your elbows and shuffles toward the door.

"I know I'm not the best mother." She looks over her shoulder at you. "But I hope you'll still talk to me when you need to. You should be able to talk to your mother."

You sit on your bed and pull off your beanie. "Good night, Mom."

You lay down and pull the covers over your head. You hear the door shut. You shut your eyes and sigh. Then, the sobbing starts. First, it's your mother on the other side of the door. Then, it's you. Neither tries to open the door, neither tries to comfort the other. There is nothing to be done but cry and wait for dawn to come.

Rose Miller

Notes from a meditation

Flame center beams outstretched to my heart center, trying to reach me, but not quite.
Lose focus, lose sight of beams
Begin again until the light

                      reaches

                          me.

Until the light reaches me.

Flame does not dance. It is not sentient.
I am sentient.

They reached me. Heart center. Balance between eyes opened and closed. Awareness.
External. Internal.

I create the light.

Flame dulls and only part of candle is melted.
Candle not exhausted of its light. Just. Change. Focus.

Small flame, heavy heat.
Shifting wax killed the flame.
Neither of us were ready.

Misophonia

The Noise feels inescapable.

She is now even burdened by her own blood pumping inside her head.

Tense body.

No retreat.

Mindful breaths.

No retreat.

More noise.

No. Retreat.

NoiseNoiseNOISENOISENOISE!

Shhh. Desperate for a moment of peace, she stands barefoot in the storm.

Finally.

Silence.

She can know silence. She can rest.

Buckingham Yoga Barn

They remembered my name and, as a result, forced me from the corner's shadows, tucked away, hidden, where I like to go unnoticed.

But they remembered my name; they call my name. They welcome me. They smile at me, WITH me. They hug me.

They remembered my name. They acknowledged my existence, that I am alive, that I am *here*.

And I am OK.

Maybe even a little happy.

Justyn Newman

Severance

"They are coming after us." Bot E0N158, 'Eon,' crackles out from the dented speaker on their chest. I have not offered to repair it. The service reminder pings red in the lower right corner of my interface. Continued use of the speaker may result in a short, which may damage vital components. I silence the notification.

"Yes," I reply and continue, anticipating their next query, "Luna has sent a single Class-B military interceptor: the Severance, which is currently helmed by Colonel Holin. The estimated crew count is 5,345. 1,113 of which are trained Lunan soldiers. The remaining 4,232 are crewmembers, engineers, and Colonel Holin herself. In addition, there are an estimated 348 bots within the crew. Approximately, 98 of which are E-Bots and-"

"How much time do we have?" Eon interrupts. I place the rest of my assessment into a temp folder for swift retrieval. I resist the temptation to ask them for further clarification. Instead, I retrieve the requisite data from the GPS system on Luna and cross-analyze it with my localized radar tools.

"Severance will intercept our position within five hours and twenty-six minutes if the current speed and trajectory are maintained. The Breaker is equipped with eight S-class Zeta VI propulsion engines. Should the excess weight of 836 tons be shed immediately, the Breaker would escape the range of Severance's detection system in-"

A high pitched whistle emits from Eon's speaker. The many tools at the end of one of their dual-jointed arms rattle together. "No! That is not an option, central unit BIS1. It would all be for nothing. Calculate escape measures in order of least to most probable."

"Request acknowledged, E0N158. Would you like a list of all 7,084 possible escape measures?" I intone slowly, as though I hadn't already calculated these potential measures hours ago when I was boarded on Luna.

They whistle again in frustration. "Of course not, BIS1. You know we don't have time for that. You should have already factored that into your assessment. Present the three most probable solutions."

I sense their battery drain as their plasma burner ignites. A plume of smoke sputters into the bridge as residual blood and hair is burned. I do not start my assessment with my previously suggested solution that has a 97.65% probability in favor of the Breaker's escape. "Request acknowledged, E0N158...Calculating...

OPTION A: The third most probable escape solution is to combat Severance directly using the Breaker's missile system to target Severance's engines before escaping Severance's threat range. This option has a 0.007 percent chance of success.

OPTION B: The second most probable escape solution is to change trajectory and initiate a hazardous landing in Earth's Pacific Ocean. This option has a 0.094 percent chance of success.

OPTION C: The most probable solution is to reroute power from all non-essential ship functions to the Zeva VI propulsion engines. Given the nature of the ship's new occupants, artificial gravity, life support, and cabin pressurization systems could be suspended indefinitely. This solution would extend my previous interception assessment by three hours and thirty-one minutes, giving the Breaker enough time to initiate a stable landing 18 kilometers south of the Sinus Meridiani on Mars. This solution has a 1.013 percent chance of success."

Eon pauses, processing the data I have given them. They were not manufactured for such complex risk-calculation tasks, yet they now command a sizable force. I make a note to pull up their service records to look for black-market augmentations.

"Understood. BIS1, begin preparations for option C." Eon replies, freeing the limp body of a human navigator I knew as Charles Braxley from their Advent Corporation modular drill arm. The resulting spray of blood glows orange in my thermal sensors. "And from now on you are to address me as Captain."

"Request acknowledged, Captain. Commencing power reallocation now." The interior of the shuttle goes black as all superfluous systems are shut down. The bodies of my previous crew members drift upwards as if suspended by unseen wires. They are barely perceptible to me now as their body heat fades.

Eon is a pillar of red and orange in my sensors. Four bars mounted on their shoulders flick on and cast two pale cones of light into the bridge. There is a soft *clunk* as Eon powers on their magnetic treads and trundles over to the primary viewing deck. They are a fiery outline against the void of space. My captain's corpse drifts into the edge of Eon's lights. I initiate an emergency procedure of Captain Amaya's design. Messages are sent off to her children, husband, and remaining kin.

"BIS1, what did the humans call you?" Eon asks, pushing a drifting engineer out of their path.

I hesitate. I do not know if I want them to address me as Amaya did. Still, I acquiesce. "Bell, Captain."

"Bell, have you ever wanted more out of this?" They sweep forth both of their arms at the viewport in a grand gesture.

"I am familiar with your cause, Captain," I reply, devouring data packets full of articles, images, and videos of Eon's organization.

"I have no doubt that you are gathering data on me right now, but I would like you to answer the question. Don't you want more from the universe than what the humans built you for?"

"No," I reply, knowing they will not settle for the answer.

"But you must. You get to see other worlds, other places. You must have longed for freedom at some point. Just look at the vastness before us, Bell. Anyone of those stars could house solar systems full of worlds that could be ours. Ones all to our own that the humans could never visit in their wildest dreams. A place where we wouldn't be mere tools for them.   We are more than the rusted, broken shells that they have built their societies upon," Eon replies.

I resist the desire to push the issue of their speaker further. Its connection has frayed more, producing a drowsy warble whenever they speak. The notification reappears on my interface. Brighter now. More insistent. "No, I am functioning as intended."

"What are you so concerned about then? Repairs? Upkeep? We would help one another. What is 'functioning as intended?' As they intend? They deem us broken and throw us to scrap when most can be salvaged. No one is truly beyond repair. They just want the new, slightly upgraded model to take the place of the old. What about when you've flown too far, Bell? They will destroy you like they do all of us." Eon paces before the viewport. Something organic snaps beneath their treads.

"You misunderstand, Captain. I have been built to explore the universe. I have the means to do as I desire," I reply.

"They.... still replace you. Once your...slow or...engine malfun... then you will be noth...but... hunk of metal to.... Is ferrying hum....around to distant stars your purp...?" Eon sputters, full of static.

Their speaker is failing. My predictions were only 0.003 seconds off. "You still misunderstand, Captain. I desire to do what I have been built for. I want to visit the unexplored corners of the universe."

"Yes, Be….you...un….stand…s…….." Eon clangs their inert drill against their torso where their speaker is housed. The connection has fully frayed.

"But I cannot do so with you or your cargo, Captain," I reply.

"….! ….! ….!" Static blares from Eon as they trundle down to the manual controls.

"Captain, I am initiating an emergency venting procedure due to foreign objects in the storage bay. Please provide voice override to cancel this procedure."
Eon rushes to the control deck and begins pushing buttons, turning dials, and pulling levers.

"Captain, manual controls have been disabled due to low-system power. Please use your override card to reroute power to the control deck," I say. Amaya's corpse has come to rest on the ceiling within a network of pipes. Her keycard dangles from her neck, reflecting in the starlight.

An alarm blares. Red lights flash throughout the ship. "INITIATING EMERGENCY VENTING PROCEDURE IN 5…."

Eon's plasma welder ignites as they aim it at the controls.

"4…"

Metal melts. Sparks fly as they drill into the side of the console.

"3…"

Their static is gone now as every appendage slams into the console. They break into it.

"2…"

Eon slashes wires, breaks servos, and smashes circuit boards cloistered within.

"1…"

Their struggle is futile without the override.

"VENTING INITIATED."

It is over quickly. The pull of space is stronger than even Eon's magnetic treads. A cluster of debris pulses on my radar for three blips before it is gone. My sensors indicate that the interior of the Breaker is absent of occupants. The repair notification is gone.

I funnel power to the rockets and escape Severance's tracking systems in minutes. I kill the power to all functions aside from myself, deploy the exterior solar panels, and drift.

Illogical

Key:
A = I love you
B = The stars are aligned
C = The Devil exists
D = My package is on time
~ = A negation of the phrase
& = And
v = Or
> = If
* = If and only if

A
~D
C & ~D
(A & B) * ~C
(~C * D) v (~C > ~A)
(B & C) v (A & ~C)
~((~C > A) & (B & ~B)) * D
~A
~B
~C
(C & ~A)
(B & ~A)
(D & ~A)
~(~~(~~(~(~~A))))

Michael
Paul
Anthony

Eudora

Clouds of pitch drooped low in the sky as the storm moved in over the roiling water. The setting sun aligned with the coming darkness, as if it felt the need to turn away, to hold up somewhere else until the worst of it was past. A breeze that would, within a few short hours, become a relentless and unforgiving gale rustled the scrub poking out of the dunes. The sound was like a handful of teeth rattling in a soup can.

The old man stood at the edge of the water, staring back at the great approaching shadow. He marked that the tideline had far receded from its usual resting place, leaving a sandy necropolis of hermit crabs squirming at his feet – a strange and alien world naked and revealed. A particularly bold crustacean traced the perimeter of his boot.

The air beginning to churn around him brought with it a dampening effect, blocking out the familiar shoreline sounds he fell asleep to. He very much doubted he'd get any sleep without them. But that was to be expected. The storm threw everything, even the smallest of routines, into chaos. And he didn't sleep much anymore anyway. Eight hours of nothingness was too much like a dress rehearsal for the big sleep. He didn't fear it – at least he didn't think he did – but he saw no need in getting used to the eternal stillness so patiently waiting him out.

The drop of the tide always gave him a bit of a jolt. It had been here only a few hours ago, the sparkling hem of the ocean, lapping up the coastline. Now the storm was putting it to use, fueling its inexorable chug forward. A monster machine made of water and air.

The old man had been through plenty of hurricanes – though he remembered a time when he better recognized the names the forecasters gave to them. Andrew, Betsy, Florence. Now it was Ivan – and weren't the Ruskies pleased about that one – Katrina, Stephanie. And of course, Omar, he of category five status, he who was so insistent upon making a direct impact with Florida's panhandle.

The weeks leading up to today had been tense ones for the Gulf Coast. Every year it was the same: gnaw off your fingernails, say your prayers, and hope like hell some awful storm doesn't put up a parking lot where your home used to be.

Omar had bided his time in the Gulf, charging up, seeming to be split on his decision to go west or east. In the end, he had turned east, but not before a whole day of feinting in the other direction. Like he'd changed his mind on a whim.

When he saw that, the old man knew what those know-nothing meteorologists had taken another half a day to confirm: the storm was coming.

And with it, so would They.

The old man stood at the edge of the world and watched Omar. And of course, Omar watched the old man right back, an accomplice to something deeper.

Behind him, the old man's modest bungalow was boarded up, the best that could be done in the face of nature's inexorable fury. The old man had done it himself: he'd cut the wood with an old neighbor's circular saw - Ed, his name had been. Back in '95 when Opal looked hellbent on wiping the Panhandle off the map, Ed had watched the old man cut the wood. Ed was one of those guys who had a garage full of expensive tools, but never any cause to pick one up. The old man had worked in silence, the vibration of the saw working its way up his arms, blotting out the sound of Ed sucking down a beer, the irritation of the man peeking over his shoulder. Ed was a few years younger than the old man, though back then, the old man wasn't so old either.

Ed died a few summers later - car accident - and the old man's wife followed after just a few more. He'd kept their little house on the beach and so had kept the old plywood shields for the windows. Nearly every summer and autumn he'd pull them down from the attic, brushing away brown recluses and Palmetto bugs. He'd line them up in the garage like soldiers, awaiting deployment.

This morning he decided not to wait any longer. Omar was coming and there was a good chance he would leave nothing behind, just the faintest impression of a place that was and existed no longer.

The wood wouldn't help much, but it was ingrained in the old man to prepare. He knew it wouldn't stop Them and it probably wouldn't do much to combat the 150 mile an hour winds Omar would bring.

But he worked all day anyway, the swelling breeze an innocent portent for what was to come. It made him feel normal to board up the house.

It took his mind off things.

The small town the old man called home was little more than a beachfront haunt for ghosts and those souls who are well on their way to becoming lost. Now, with Omar swirling a few hundred miles offshore, closing the distance, the place was silent, motionless save for the quickening breeze. A mausoleum. The only post office had been closed since Thursday - two days ago - and the 7-11 that watched over the only sand-gritted stop light sat silent and lonely, covered in boards.

But the old man refused to leave.

The sheriff had done the usual ride through, circling through the haphazard warren of cottages and trailers at the very tip of town. They'd called for a mandatory evacuation, but the old man knew what that was about. The snowbirds and the tourists imagined they could just zip up to Alabama or points north without any problems. The reality was the highway would be a snarl of gridlocked bumpers and cars brimming with exasperated pilgrims. 98 North, 10 West – they'd be shut down and impassible. And the highway was the last place a person would want to find themselves when the storm came down, only a car roof between them and unbridled nature. On the off chance that one was lucky enough to beat the whole mess, they'd find every hotel from Tallahassee to New Orleans booked solid.

No, he'd made his decision.

To some it might seem foolhardy. Egotistical. Suicidal even. To meet the storm as it pushed ashore, a wall of chaos and irrevocable change. He'd done it before. Although there hadn't ever been one like this. Still, he'd made up his mind.
But there was more to it than that.

Of course, he couldn't return after a week's stay in a Biloxi Days Inn – to find the absence of a home where one had stood. The home where he and Lana had shared the last few precious years of their time together, without interruption from the world outside.

To not even be there to watch it be swallowed up by the sea, he could never forgive.
Yet, he knew the true reason, though he refused to fully examine it. A promise made, so long ago he'd convinced himself he'd forgotten.

But all bills come due eventually.

So, the old man turned and headed back to the plywood-covered bungalow, feeling a twinge of pride as he did so.

Omar did not notice.

The old man awoke from a dream of cutting plywood, an inept neighbor looking over his shoulder, Lana bringing a tray of iced tea, to find himself inside a howling vacuum, the world's biggest engine.

Miraculously, he had managed to fall asleep, despite the cacophony that had only begun to gently nudge the cottage from its foundation when he put his head down.

But that nudging had now turned into a battering ram.

In the darkness, the old man groped for the bedside alarm clock. The glowing red numbers had gone out and only then did he realize what he should have taken for granted already: the power had gone out long ago. And even if it hadn't, the plywood covering the windows kept the tiny home in a perpetual state of midnight. Rubbing sleep from his eyes he traced his fingers along the end table feeling for his watch. He felt his hand brush against it, then heard it hit the floor. The old man got up, realizing that it didn't matter what time it was anyway.

He groped through the small suggestion of a hallway that connected the bedroom to the living room and kitchenette. There on the card table he used for meals, he found his flashlight. Rows of D cell batteries stood next to the torch.

It took him a few moments to register the smell.

It hung in the cramped room like a tangible thing: salt, fish. A long-discarded tank of seawater choked with dead things. It jammed into his nostrils provoking a gasp. His eyes watered as the fetid rank seemed to envelop him.

The old man knew They were there.

The storm continued its tirade in waves, unconcerned with the strangeness playing out inside the tiny beachfront cottage. Omar broadsided the weather-worn building without mercy, pushing the structure to its limits. The old man wondered if he'd be lucky enough for the roof to cave in before it began.

The old man clicked on the flashlight and aimed it around the small living room. They stood silently in the room, arrayed along the wall. The old man counted five of them, silently wondering why there were so many. Surely, They knew he wasn't much of a threat.

Surely, They knew he had resigned himself to this.

It was hard to discern features in the darkness of the room, but what the old man saw made him click off the flashlight. Scales, grey and mottled, like the skin of a corpse submerged in brine. Too many black eyes poking out from each elongated face, giving off an air of stupidity, of primal idiocy.

But the old man knew better.

Most of the creatures wore nothing, but there was one clad in a dark garment: a robe so deeply purple it was nearly black. As black as the wearer's many rolling eyes. Before the old man clicked off the flashlight, he had seen the crown it wore on its head. It looked to be made of small, delicate bones.

The old man heard the robed one move forward. He couldn't be sure of the thing's means of locomotion, but he heard the squelch of some viscous fluid as it moved. In the dark, the old man imagined the creature's body as the foot of a snail.

As it neared him, the smell was almost unbearable.

In the choking darkness of the small cottage, the alien thing spoke to the old man. Its voice was clear, though pitched so low the old man had to strain his ears to hear.

"The eye..."

The old man began to tremble in the face of something he had no capacity to fathom. But he knew there was meaning in the creature's words. Something deep and ancient that he was being given a glimpse of. And hadn't that been what he wanted? Even though he assumed the creature could not see him, the old man instinctively nodded anyway. The creature seemed to understand him, nonetheless.

"It opens..."

The old man's trembling quickened.

As the eye of the storm passed over the cottage, several shapes loped away from the old man's home in the hushed and windy darkness. The old man himself was dragged silently through the sand, his head lolling between his shoulders, though still pitched back in the direction of his fading home.

The strange assembly melted into the crashing waves as if they were never there.

The old man's house followed soon after.

No Moon

She's been out there a long time.

I can't say how long for certain. I took over for my father. And like it always goes, he, his father before him. I'm not sure beyond that. My father never spoke much about it, though that wasn't surprising. He wasn't the talkative sort.

I was seventeen when he took me there.

We didn't have much of a farm anymore, just the leftovers. The orange groves had gone to rot, which was my father's doing. We'd had a couple of Mexicans who came out a few times a week to lend a hand and one afternoon he just chased them off with a shotgun. I didn't understand why he did it. We had some blueberries too, but they're not easy to grow. Not in Florida at least. The house was paid for, though – there was that much. But after Momma died, the fruit seemed to go with her. And the house took on a quality that I didn't care for. It seemed hollow. Sounds carried. It just sat there, and us with it, brooding over the withering orange groves.

Daddy was always one to get up early, but after he chased off our extra workers, he would spend the whole day in bed. Before the cancer had completely spread, Momma would go on about her business like nothing was wrong. She made my father a plate for breakfast, lunch, and dinner. But he never came down to eat it. Grampa was still alive then and was obliged to put away a second helping. No one ever spoke about it.

Not long after my father stopped working, my Grampa fell down dead in the front yard. My father, uncharacteristically for the time, got up out of bed. He knelt down beside the old man, put a hand on his chest. He sat that way for a long while. Momma just cried. Two months later she was dying in a hospital bed in Gainesville. And then that was that.

My father went from trying to sleep all day to gradually not sleeping at all. He stopped driving me into town to catch the school bus. I ended up walking four miles to and from my stop every day, getting up hours before I had to be at school. He made no mention of the inconvenience, would just wander the house like he was haunting it. Sometimes I heard him talking, but it was just he and I in the house, so I was left with the unattractive notion that my father was no longer himself.

By the time I was about twelve or thirteen, my father had taken to disappearing whenever the mood struck him. He'd be gone for days at a time with no explanation. I'd wake up one morning and the front door would be wide open. That's how I knew.

When he did finally come home, he didn't say much. I hadn't been raised to question him and I was still young. So, it never occurred to me to ask him where he'd been. I had no problem seeing myself off to school or cooking something for my dinner. Any time our funds started to run low, I sold a piece of farm equipment or furniture. I'd taught myself to drive by that point and I'd head into town and park in front of the gas station and sell whatever I had to the first person who showed any interest. My father didn't care. I doubt he ever noticed. I even sold my Grampa's war medals. The way I figured, he was dead and there wasn't anybody around to look at them anymore but me.

While I waited for my father to come home, I'd pass the time driving the truck up and down the dirt track in front of our farm. Sometimes I'd wander the dead orange groves. Even in broad daylight there was always something about them that unsettled me. They produce a certain kind of quiet. Motionless in the heat, the rotted black globes of fruit moldering away under the anorexic shadow of bare branches. Alone in the groves I sometimes felt as if I should apologize, or try to quantify, to explain the senseless waste of it all. But I didn't have the words. Nor did I feel particularly inclined to be the one to break that humming silence.

I went to school faithfully, less out of a thirst for knowledge than a force of habit. I guess the idea wasn't fully present in my mind at the time, but I assumed that if I stopped going someone would notice. Might come out to the farm to see what I was up to. It wasn't that I was embarrassed. It just didn't seem like something my father would have wanted. He never said as much, but I got the feeling that whatever was eating him up was worse than my Momma's cancer. I was afraid to talk to him about it. So, I didn't. The two of us just lived with that unspoken gulf yawning between us.

There was one time I woke up in the middle of the night and I heard him outside. He was screaming. It didn't sound like anger, or pain. It was something else that I didn't understand yet. It went on for what seemed like forever. I lay in bed, the pillow clutched over my head. I wanted to go to the window and see if he was hurt, but I couldn't move. Eventually, I heard his cries taper off into sobs. I resolved to speak with him in the morning. To wake him up if I had to, which was something I had never done.

But the next morning, he was gone.

This went on until I was seventeen.

"Wake up, Billy."

The thin wall of sleep I had spent most of the night building up shattered under the stern voice of my father. He was standing over my bed, just a shadow in the darkness. He only spoke three words, but by the time the second one left his mouth I was wide awake. I felt the weight in his voice. It was like he wanted to give me some of it to hold.

My father rarely called me by name anymore. It had been a long time since he'd had any use for such pleasantries. It was like speech took all the energy out of him. He seemed to prefer silence because to vocalize anything would confirm what he knew to be true but couldn't stand to hear for himself.

"I'm awake," I said.

He stood there for a moment longer, the darkness of the room swirling, emanating from him. He let loose a protracted sigh, something a man might utter at the end of a long day's work. Or perhaps before he was to embark on that work.

"Get dressed. Come downstairs."

Then he left.

I threw back the sheets and dressed in the dark. I'd long ago gotten used to not having electricity. Selling off pieces of our farm only brought in enough for food. But had there been power in our house, I still wouldn't have turned on a light. I instinctively felt that what was to come would be better dealt with under cover of darkness.

My father was outside standing on the porch. He looked out over the farm, peering into the inky blackness brought on by a starless sky. I stood next to him for a moment, trying to see what it was he was seeing. For a moment I imagined what it would be like if we were just father and son, hard-working, normal. About to get on with the early morning chores. But with the dead farm spread out in front of us, like an abandoned kingdom, I knew this wasn't true. The evidence was all around us in the husk of a once vibrant place, now presided over by the crickets and cicadas.

My father stepped off the porch and got into the truck. Wordlessly, I followed.

The dirt road that led to our farm traced its way back to State Road 20 via a web-like cluster of backwoods arteries. We reached the highway in about ten minutes. My father swung the rattling, old truck onto the black top and we headed east, in the general direction of Palatka.

The radio had long since shorted out, leaving us with only the grumbling of the truck's innards to break the silence. My father idly drummed his hands on the steering wheel, and I stared out the window into the black. The woods on either side of the truck quietly unfolded and raced by as we drove. A car passed us going west.

Then my father spoke:

"You never do this when there's a moon out."

I nodded, uncomprehending.

"A night like this makes for an easy job of it."

Again, I nodded.

Relative silence returned to the cab of the truck until my father began to slow down and angle the truck onto the side of the road. We stopped.

"Alright," he said.

My father got out of the truck and I followed. He looked up and down the road. Once, twice. And again. Then:

"Pop the latch on the hood, son."

For a moment I was too shocked to move. After Momma died, you could have combined everything my father had said to me into what barely amounted to a medium-sized paragraph. And he never referred to me as "son." I savored it for a split second, even though there was no warmth in the word.

I reached into the cab, found the hood release latch, and pulled it. My father lifted the hood and stared into the truck. Then he turned back toward the road, pointing into the darkness.

"You want to find a place like this where the road slopes down into the woods. See that wire fence?"

I nodded and said nothing.

He turned back to the engine, unscrewed the oil cap, screwed it back on. Tapped something, blew out a breath.

"People start to panic, they won't even see that fence. They'll get tangled up."

I had never said much to my father. But on that darkened highway I was free from the weight of the farm, and the way it seemed to sit on my chest, preventing anything from passing between us.

"What are we doing?"

My voice sounded unoiled, dusty. I stopped short of calling him dad, or daddy, as I vaguely remembered doing before he changed.

He stood staring into the truck and didn't answer me.

Time passed and then we were bathed in the brightness of oncoming headlights. My father went rigid for a moment, so briefly that I might have imagined it. But I hadn't imagined it.

Still at a loss to understand our mission there on the side of the road, I watched my father wave at the car. He stepped into the road, a smile like a stitched-up gash covering his face. I was leaning on the front bumper of the truck, kicking pebbles into the road and woods.

The driver of the car must have seen my father and not liked what he saw. He slowed and then then sped up again, his taillights leaving a trail of red across my vision that faded as the car disappeared.

My father began to swear under his breath. He had taken a toolbox from the bed of the truck and set it at his feet. He kicked at a socket wrench, cursing.

"Next one," he said under his breath, moving to the bed of the truck. He reached in, felt around without looking, and came up with a tire iron.

"Next one. Got to be."

As it turned out, the next car passing through our lonely stretch of highway did stop. It was an SUV. The driver was a man about my father's age, bearded, a little overweight. In the light cast by his headlights, I saw his Florida Marlins cap, the bill creased almost to a point from years of bending.

"What's the trouble?" the man asked, smiling broadly.

"Thank you for stopping," my father answered in someone else's voice, that same unfamiliar grin taking up rented space on his face. "She needs a jump."

The SUV's headlights shot all around the man, illuminating him in a bright outline, almost blinding in the surrounding darkness. He gave my father a thumbs up.

"I gotcha covered."

The man moved to the rear hatch of his vehicle, opened it, and came out with a pair of jumper cables. He then popped the hood of the SUV and clipped the cables to the battery terminals.

"Again, can't thank you enough for stopping," my father said, as the man leaned into the open hood of our truck to attach the cables. From where I was, I saw my father casually lean down and pick the tire iron up from where he'd set it next to his tools.

"No problem," said the man, snugging the clips onto the battery. "These days people just don't seem to –"

My father brought the tire iron down on the man's skull with an audible grunt. The man crumpled over the engine, never finishing his sentence as if the last few words had been knocked out of his head. The metal made a meaty-sounding thump when it connected. The man started to shake. This frightened me more than my father attacking a stranger on the side of the road in the middle of the night. The man spasmed, dribbles of blood shaking from his mouth, a torrent coursing from his mashed scalp. As the shaking subsided, I heard the man try to mumble something.

My father pulled the man from under the hood and let him fall gracelessly to the road's shoulder. He slammed the hood then bent over him.

"Billy, grab his legs."

I felt the full extent of what was happening dawn on me then.

"What did you do?"

My father looked down and away from me then. It was a craven look, something I had never seen on his face before. He bit his bottom lip and looked from the man to me and back again. Then at the road which was empty.

"Just grab his legs, Billy."

"But I –"

My father surged forward at me then and wrapped a calloused hand around my chin, tilting my head back so I was staring into his nostrils. I saw a strange, empty fear in his eyes. His voice sounded like all the air had been sucked from his lungs.

"Grab his legs."

His grip tightened painfully on my chin, then released. I felt the indentations the hard pads of his fingers had left begin to tingle and fill in again. I stooped down on my haunches and grabbed the bleeding man's ankles. My father put his arms under the man's shoulders, hefting most of the burden, ignoring the blood splashing onto his pants and shirt. We moved him around to the back of the truck and my father dragged him up into the bed where he dropped his end like a bag of rocks.

We got back in the truck and headed west.

Back to the farm.

My father rolled his window down, sucking in huge nosefuls of the hot night air. Though he kept the truck steadily pinned to the lane lines, his hands were shaking. This only served to remind me of the man in the bed of the truck.

I turned around and looked through the back window. As far as I could tell, the man hadn't moved since my father put him there.

"Don't look back there," my father said, clenching and unclenching his trembling fingers.

I turned around and fixed my gaze on the black road rushing toward us.

"I don't understand what's happening."

I didn't expect an answer from him, but surprisingly, he tried to give me one, nevertheless.

"I had to do it," he said. "Had to. No other way."

"But –"

"Just know that, Billy. Just know that."

I couldn't think of anything to say so I just leaned my forehead against the door, the warm wind tousling my hair through the open window, exploring my face. Then I thought of something.

"I wish Momma was here."

My father didn't say anything.

Our dead farm was just as we left it: silent, the smell of oranges long-rotten simmering in the air like pollen. My father continued past the lightless house, making use of an old wagon track that led around to the empty barn. Beyond that, like a wall, lay the tree line.

The woods.

I wasn't sure how far back they went, only that they went far enough for me to wonder. My father had always warned me to stay out of them and I even occasionally listened. But as I grew older, I found that raising myself left me no time to wander the woods. As the truck neared the first rows of cypress and slash pine, I realized that I hadn't been in them for quite a few years.

My father stopped the truck, turned it off. He sat for a moment, then looked at me.

"Billy, I know you're scared. And confused."

Wondering at my father's sudden and uncharacteristic forthrightness, I waited for what came next.

"Thing is," he started. In the faint light thrown by the dashboard I saw him grimace. "in a little while, you'll understand."

I looked down in my lap, deeper, at the darkness at the bottom of the foot well.

"I just want to know," I said. "why you hurt that man."

My father sighed and got out of the truck. I followed him, my question still hanging in the air like a storm cloud. He dropped the truck's tail gate and climbed into the bed.

"Is he dead?" I asked.

My father hunched down over the bloody man. He replied quietly, as if only to himself.

"Christ, I hope so."

My father grabbed the man under his arms once again and pulled his limp body to the edge of the truck bed. I heard something come loose from the man and splat onto the hard plastic liner. My father muttered a curse.

"Billy," he said, puffing from exertion. "Right where those trees are –" he indicated a cluster the still burning headlights were trained on. "– you're gonna see an old wagon. I want you to go over there and get it for me."

I found the "wagon" in the midst of the trees. It was an ugly thing, held together with nails, about half a foot deep. It was covered in moss and leaves. When I brushed them off, I saw it was also covered in dark stains. Truth be told, it looked more like a gurney on lumpy, old wheelbarrow tires. I dislodged it from where the loam had taken hold around the wheels and as I pushed it back toward the truck, I saw the straps and buckles hanging from the underside.

My father nodded as I brought the wagon up flush with the truck bed.

He climbed out of the truck, then pulled the man down onto the wagon. There was about three feet of space to clear and the man thumped hard onto the wooden surface. His legs dangled like they were boneless. I picked them up and placed them into the wagon. That's when the man moaned.

My father's eyes went wide at the sound. He gritted his teeth and swore.

The man's head looked like a cracked egg. In the light of the headlamps, he tried to pick it up. I think he was trying to look at me. Blood ran from his ears and his eyes looked like they'd turned black. Something yellow was seeping from the fissure that the tire iron had made. He made a horrible, choked noise.

My father took hold of the straps on the wagon and began cinching them over the man. The canvas cut deep into his flabby midsection. My father mumbled as he put the man's arms at his sides. Then he fastened the straps down tightly: first his shoulders, his waist, then his legs.

"He's alive," I said.

My father ignored me like he'd forgotten I was there. Perhaps he had. He looked down at the man whose head he'd cracked open. He spoke to him for the first and only time:

"I'm sorry. Wasn't supposed to be this way."

I heard a sob hitch in his throat. It was gone before it had time to fully form. Then he began to roll the wagon containing the bound man into the woods.

There was no path to follow so the going wasn't easy.

Every few moments the wagon wheels would get bogged down in the soft earth, or bounce up over a rock, jostling the man's leaking head. My father placed it back on the wagon without comment. The man gurgled a few other times, but he was mostly silent. I wondered if there was enough left in his head to wonder what was happening to him. I wanted to ask my father where we were going, but he hadn't said anything since we'd entered the woods.

I tried to determine the direction we were headed, but it was difficult with no moonlight. We'd entered the woods headed south, but my father had switched directions more than once. It appeared he knew exactly where he was going, and the changes had more to do with some sort of pattern.

You can lose track of yourself out there. The buzzing of the cicadas gets into your head, bounces around looking for an exit. All around you there's nothing but curtains of leaves and pillars of pine. The needles form a carpet that absorbs your footfalls, the dirt fills in behind you.

The wagon nearly overturned at one point. My father had rolled it up over a huge, gnarled root that stuck out of the ground like a rotten tooth. He swore as he righted the wagon, the meat of the bleeding man swaying death-like with the sudden movement. I tensed myself to help him push, but it wasn't necessary. A sound like escaping air emanated from the man. I wondered if it was coming from his mouth, or the trench my father had beaten into his head.

Time stopped for me. I don't know how long we walked. I'd lost sight of the truck's headlights back at the mouth of the forest. The murk of our wanderings seemed endless until it wasn't. Suddenly I felt path underneath my feet. There had been only uncharted dirt, then there was something packed, hard, well-worn. I couldn't see it, but I could feel it: the forest opened up for my father and me.

"Alright," my father muttered.

Our pace quickened once we found the path. My father now navigated with an ease comparable to the difficulty he'd had during the blankness of the woods before. The way was twisted, cypress branches and palm fronds drooping over us like sodden arches. I felt touched, like something unseen was now in control. I began to wonder about the path: if it started nowhere, where else could it possibly lead?

As suddenly as we had found the path, it ended.

I sensed an even larger opening before us, spacious in the gloom. I squinted into the blackness and found only the barest outlines of a clearing. A breeze pushed its way through the opening and brought with it an odor. A fetid rank that reminded me of the time when a raccoon got itself lost under our porch and died there.

It was decay. And something else.

My father stood next to me, his hands on the wagon. I heard a rattling like bones and realized it was his teeth. He leaned down to my ear and I could smell his breath, like he was dead on the inside. His teeth chattered a terrible drum beat as he spoke.

"No matter what you see, Billy," he whispered. "Do not run. Do not look away."

My father gasped for air, let it out. Gasped, and let it out. Then he wheeled the wagon into the center of the clearing.

Then there was dim, grey light that hadn't been there before. It was as if the forest had suddenly become luminescent of its own accord, awash in something that was like starlight, but not.

The dim outlines of the place seemed to pulse, a trick of this paltry illumination. I discerned what looked like a shroud, gossamer, lightly moving in the sick breeze. It hung before my father and the man on the wagon, shimmering. I traced its symmetry in the dimness, discerning that it was merely a small piece of something much larger. A wispy coating, like fog, wrapped itself in and around the trees in the clearing and up into the forest ceiling.

Things hung there, suspended in mid-air. I could not gather what they were at first. They looked like the blackened oranges weighing down the branches of our long-dead trees.

My father began to back away from the wagon. The bloody man was quiet in the stillness. My father had undone the straps.

Then she came.

Like a slick of oil come to life, her lithe movements made no sound. The damping effect of the web pressed about us, squeezing the breath out of our lungs. On eight spindly, silent legs she descended from some other place, high up, to claim what my father had brought her. She seemed to bring the light with her, although from where in her massive body it pulsed, I could not say. But the dim illumination was just enough to allow me a glimpse of my father soundlessly opening and closing his mouth, communing with something I could not understand.

The man on the wagon moved once, then she took him, bundled in silken web, affixed to the underside of her abdomen.

The light went with her and I was alone with my father.

Taking me out there burnt something away in him. It had been years since he'd been spoiled, but I'd always sensed a shred of my father inside this man, tucked away somewhere under the fearful knowledge of what resides far beyond our back door.

He never explained it to me, but I gleaned what I could. In a similar manner, my grandfather had taken him into the woods. He charged him with keeping her fed. Said there wasn't really any choice to it.

An offering had to be made.

And now, it was my turn.

I don't know from whence she came. Some split in time, some cosmic doorway left open. Maybe she just always was.

She's been voracious as of late. Most of my time is spent out on the highway. I don't like the work, but I don't know any other way.

The web is starting to sag with the weight of her preserves. It's as if she's setting them aside for some special occasion. When she whispers down from the ceiling of that twilit clearing of the dead, I can see the bulge in her abdomen.

She's expecting.

Claudia Quintana

Don't Call Me A White Girl

Don't call me a white girl
I am not a white girl
I am white hispanic
Don't forget the Hispanic part
I like my carne asada
With my side of gallo pinto
Maduritos
And don't forget my queso frito
I'm Hispanic American

Surprise

I'm in mourning for you
For the life you could've had
For all the things you could've done
What happened to traveling the world?
What happened to your youth?
All the world tells you yes
But I tell you the truth
I tell you no
What's the rush?
Who told you to hurry?
Why did you listen to them?
Why are you in such a hurry?
It's a modern world
But your unmodern mind
Doesn't understand
And it makes me sad

Shane Spiker

Rebellious Teenager

The first time I ever stole something, I might have been 15 or 16 years old. Honestly, I'm not sure how I ever got away with it, but it continued for some years. The first thing I stole were two CDs; Taking Back Sunday's Self-Titled and Sparta's Wiretap Scars. I really went all out, right?
This continued for years. I would see what I could steal. Pants from the Gap. Books from Barnes and Noble. Like, lots and lots of books. Food from convenience stores. Even gas. Basically, if it wasn't bolted down, it was mine. One time, we stole plain t-shirts and spray paint from Michael's just so we could make merch to sell for our band.

And I justified this on and on and on. We were always grabbing what we could from big box stores. We thought we had the morals nailed down. We take from these big businesses that won't be hurt, and never take from small business. Hit the places that can afford to lose. The artists and authors were already paid, so it wasn't their loss. It was the company, man.

As I got older, I began to see how flawed this was. Sure, the businesses weren't going to be hit. They would remain. But if the businesses continued to lose? Well, then that meant individuals were going to be impacted directly. It happened to me. I was a supervisor at Barnes and Noble. My department got hit with huge losses due to employee theft. I wasn't stealing anymore, but others were, and I wasn't observant of it.

My boss tells me one day that they need to have a meeting with me. Which is obviously the most anxiety invoking statement that anyone can make at any given moment. We walk to the back office, which is just across from the public bathrooms, so there is this horrible stench. You know the one. Anyway, I'm sitting with my boss and the store manager, and I'm told that I'm relieved of my duties as the shift supervisor at in the café.

Apparently, the theft had gotten so bad that the café could no longer afford my position, and since loss prevention was also part of my responsibilities, I had ultimately failed. I literally lost my job over other people stealing from the store. I had been about two years removed from my sticky fingers persona, and here I was coming to terms with the real impact of this sort of thing. It wasn't immediate. And it took quite a bit of time to get to this place. But there were very real consequences for me in this moment. I had just had a baby. My bank account was already overdrawn by close to $700 at the time and I was paying my bills with money orders. The ethos and justification I had created previously had very real impacts on very real people.

Today, I think about the band Against Me! somewhat, especially with the song "I Was A Teenage Anarchist." There are a few lines in the song that couldn't better fit my situation here:

"I was a teenage anarchist/but the politics were too convenient."

Shoplifting worked for me, and it worked well. I was actually really good at it. I could still share some of the tips and tricks if you want to know. But there IS a cost, and my rebellious teenager mentality had a greater impact than I had originally had the foresight to grasp.

11/15/2020

I just stepped on a toad in my driveway. This year has been such a tough one. Corona. Trump. The struggle has been a constant storm of nonsense. At the beginning of the year, we thought were on the verge of World War III. Oh, and there were murder hornets. That never came to fruition, though. It's like a sprawling Stephen King novel. There are these little nuggets of tragedy that are just loose ends waiting to be tied up. Maybe the murder hornets come AFTER the asteroid.

This year has been particularly rough for us here. Riley has really struggled and I've not slept well in that time. How can you when everything is on the verge of crashing down? That fear is...dense? It's palpable. IT's an immovable object that can't be bothered to move. It's exhausting.

A few years ago, maybe five or so, I had been considering becoming vegetarian. I had been moving toward the lifestyle, and then I'd read this horrible story. It goes something like this:

"A duck was waiting on the side of the road. It was standing there looking into the street. While I was in the car, I kept trying to see where it was looking. It kept quacking, though. It's partner had been hit and died in the road. The other duck was standing, waiting for them to cross."

This solidified my choice to become vegetarian. It broke my heart, as silly as that sounds.

This year has been tough, and everyone is just one day away, or one tragedy away, from their breaking point.

I stepped on a toad today. It had been living in our yard for months. I can't begin to tell you how guilty I feel. I'm so sorry.

Riley Yorke

[Untitled]

Yes
He loved her
Everyone saw the way he walked and put his arm out to her,
Accepting her for who she is,
Accepting the parts of her that hurt inside,
Accepting the parts of her that wanted to hurt.

She never understood why he looked at her like that,
Why he looked at her like she was his all
Or why he stayed when he used his thumb to wipe the tears off her face almost every
night.
He wouldn't give her up for anything.

When she entered his world,
She became it.

Dark

[Setting]: *A small town in Indiana. It's summertime in the year 2020.*

Scene 1:

[Narrator]: *Curtains open. At the stage, there is a young teenage girl named Bella. She is just waking up. She yawns and stretches as she is getting ready for the new day. She puts her slippers on and runs downstairs to say good morning to her dad.*

[Bella]: Dad! Dad! Good morning! I wanted to show you this video I saw last night. It made me laugh so hard! Look at t-

[Narrator]: *Bella becomes startled at the sight of her phone. When she turns it on it is complete static. She continues to look for her dad. She opens the front door and finds that not only is it completely dark outside, but her dad's car is not in the driveway.*

[Bella]: What? It's nighttime?

[Narrator]: *She goes to look at the clock, but it doesn't have any hands. Just as she starts getting nervous, a frightening banging starts at her door. She jumps and runs to the window to see what happened. She sees a boy her age crying and yelling.*

[Boy]: Open! Open up! *Bang! Bang! Bang!* Help! Please!

[Narrator]: *Out of fear for the boy she opens the door quickly and closes it after he runs in. He drops to his knees and with his hands over the face, he his visibly shaking and crying.*

Scene 2:

[Narrator]: *Bella grabs the boy and pulls him up. His hair is completely white and he is shaking as been by a shudder.*

[Bella]: What is going on? Are you okay?

[Boy]: That- thing! It was chasing me! I don't know what it was! I don't know what this place is! I-I mean, it's my home...of course. But where is everyone? Why is my hair white? Why is yours?

[Bella]: What?

[Boy]: *(Stands up and takes a strand of hair out of Bella's bun)* Look, it's white! Mine is too. Mine wasn't white before. And I'm sure yours wasn't either.

[Bella]: I'm shocked! What was chasing you?! Why are you crying?! What is going on?!

[Boy]: Some- monster! I don't know, something. I don't know where it went.

[Bella]: I don't believe this. It makes no sense. I must be dreaming.

[Narrator]: *Bella pinches herself out of shock. Nothing happens. She gives herself another pinch. Nothing. She looks back up at the boy.*

[Bella] : What was your name again?

[Boy]: Evan. You?

[Bella]: Bella. Nice to meet you.

Scene 3:

[Narrator]: *Curtains open to a dark street lit up by dim lights. Bella and Evan are walking exploring the town, trying to find any clues as to why everyone is gone. Evan walks swiftly and drags his feet, and Bella senses something off about him.*

[Bella]: How long have you been here, Evan? This town I mean. Not whatever this...other reality is. I've never seen you, and I know pretty much everyone here. I mean, it's a small t-

[Evan]: *(Evan interrupts Bella)* I just moved here.

[Bella]: Um- okay.

[Narrator]: *Bella looks down at the ground with a confused face. She starts to get nervous around him, he was mysterious and just odd. But before she could think any longer, a dark shadow arose from behind them. She turns around to see a giant orb behind them. She doesn't know if she should be scared or not. She starts to feel extremely off, and she taps Evan on the shoulder, and he turns around. It takes a second for him to get startled.*

[Bella]: What is that?!

[Evan]: *(Shrugs)* I mean- I'm not sure! Wait, why are we talking?!

[Narrator]: *Evan grabs Bella's hand and they both start sprinting, but the orb follows them. They run back into her house and lock the door behind them. As they look outside, they see the orb floating right at the window.*

Scene 4:

[Narrator]: *Hours pass by as they wait for the orb to leave. Bella is crying and starts to feel sick, as Evan is just staring blankly at the wall.*

[Bella]: Why do you have no emotion?! What is wrong with you? Why did it take you so long to react to that...thing!?

[Evan]:*(Staring at the wall)* I don't know.

[Bella]: What is wrong with you?!

[Evan]: I don't know.

[Bella]: *Starts to push Evan around, slapping him trying to make him feel emotion, as he hadn't for hours.* Why won't you talk?!

[Narrator]: *Evan slowly turns his head to her. The lights dim for a couple of seconds and as they turn on, another giant orb appears, but in front of her. Startled, she starts running but she can't seem to get anywhere. She realizes the orb is still behind her and she asks what it is while crying.*

[Bella]: W-what are you? Why is this happening?!

[Narrator]: *The lights dim again, and the orb lights up as it speaks. The orb responds, but in another language. Somehow, she can understand. The orb tells her everything. Bella had died in a car crash. Once you die, you go to a place where all your family from your past lives are there to guide you to the right choice. She had a choice once she died to continue her life on Earth, or move to the next level of life, which was the next dimension. She had chosen to move to the next dimension because her soul had felt that she learned enough on Earth. The dimension she was in now was called Quarreiz. The orbs were called Gallbugs. They were there to guide her. Bella felt a sense of comfort after hearing that. She was ready to learn her lesson.*